"Who's responsible for this?" the general roared. He held up one of the pink grapefruit he'd discovered in a box of grenades.

A major moved forward, stepped on a grapefruit, and fell to the ground, spraining his ankle. He was the first casualty of the annual war games. A captain rushed up to help the fallen man, tripped over two jumbo oranges and rocketed into the air, coming down with a thud on three more grapefruit, squishing the juices straight into the blinded eyes of three lieutenants.

The general viewed the battlefield with dismay. One major, one captain and three lieutenants lay felled in the Battle of the Citrus Fruit. About them, immobilized, stood a company of battle-trained Marines, afraid to move forward into the juicy minefield.

Soaked in fruit juice, boiling with fury, the general was determined to find the enemy. And who should it turn out to be but one of his own troops, by the name of Gomer Pyle. . . .

GOMER PYLE,
U.S.M.C.

•

E. KITZES KNOX

PYRAMID BOOKS • NEW YORK

GOMER PYLE, U.S.M.C.

A PYRAMID BOOK
First printing, December 1965

Printed in the United States of America

PYRAMID BOOKS are published by Pyramid Publications, Inc.
444 Madison Avenue, New York, N.Y. 10022, U.S.A.

Chapter One

THE LATE AFTERNOON SUN caught the specks of dust floating lazily to the wooden barracks floor and turned them into diamond sparklers. The same warm sun was in Marine recruit Gomer Pyle's eyes and made him squint.

Gomer shifted just enough so that the sun missed his eyes, but not enough to stop the sun from glancing off his teeth which were exposed in a smile. He had only the standard thirty-two teeth, including the one which had grown in snaggled, but you could never convince a casual observer of that. Gomer's teeth were so large and shiny that they gave the impression of being great in number. At the moment, the reflection from Gomer's smile could have picked up a blinker receiving station on a distant hill had there been one.

"It just ain't so, fellers," Gomer Pyle was saying, as he leaned back on his bunk. "It just ain't so," he insisted, still smiling and squinting and revealing even more of his mouthful of teeth because of the double task of smiling and squinting at the same time.

"Oh, it is too so, Gomer," said the smallish young man in the rumpled utilities, who was sitting near by on an equally rumpled bunk. "People don't care about a serviceman today. People don't care about servicemen unless there's a war. A hot war, I mean."

A general rumble of approval rolled around the barracks where the members of the platoon were lying, sitting, and sprawling out in various poses of apathy and boredom. The flies that strayed in for a late afternoon snack enjoyed the visit; the men were just too forlorn to brush them off. A few gnats drifted in like smoke, hovered, found no challenge and nothing fermenting, so they drifted away again to look for excitement in the garbage area.

It was quite evident that morale in the barracks left something to be desired. The something was mail.

The smallish young man next to Gomer Pyle expelled a large sigh which rippled in his shirt front. His name was Regis, but Gomer called him "Ray" because that was short for Gomer's pronunciation. In Gomer's mouth "Regis" came out "Ray-jis."

"Nobody could care less," said Regis, who seemed to possess the only energy source flowing through the dejected barracks. "Who wants to write to a Marine when he isn't fighting a war?"

"Aw, now, Ray. You know for a fact that ain't true. I seen you get some mail just today."

Ray, alias Regis, rolled his far apart eyes so that the irises almost bobbed out of sight. "From my mother. From my mother. I got a letter from my mother!"

Gomer's smile, which was more vertical than horizontal, lengthened with delight. "Well, now wasn't that sweet of her. What'd she say?"

Regis, alias Ray, crimped up his mouth and pulled a face. "Crabgrass. That's what she said. She said it was too bad I was here in training so that she and Dad didn't have any help pulling up the crabgrass. You see what I mean," he shot a glance around the despondent assemblage. "All she's thinking about is crabgrass."

Gomer massaged his own crewcut head with his knuckles. "Well, parents is of a different generation."

Ray sighed again because his natural bent was toward pessimism. "Gomer," he said, "you love everybody."

"I do not," said Gomer. "I do not love everybody. I don't love Sgt. Carter. I like him, but I don't love him."

It was Jim Holmes who spoke up now. Jim was a big

lad from New York. He was still amazed at the way Gomer could drag his one syllable name into three syllables.

"Gomer," boomed Jim in a loud voice, "the point is that you don't see anything bad about people. You excuse everything. As far as you're concerned, nobody ever does anything wrong."

Gomer Pyle shook his head. "Aw, now, that isn't so, Ja-uh-um. Now take my cousin Marthie. She used to make change in the collection plate in church every Sunday. You know, she'd put in a quarter and take out fifteen cents. Only one Sunday, I seen her put in a quarter and take out thirty-five cents, and that's wrong! And I told her so. I said: 'Cousin Marthie, that's wrong. I seen you steal from the Lord.' But she didn't see it as wrong. She said the Lord had seen to it that potato bugs ate up a big chunk of her 'tater profits and she said she had some change coming. She didn't MEAN no harm, but it was wrong all the same."

The original spokesman for the disgruntled found his tongue. "How'd we get off on that?" he yelped. "I'm just saying that we don't get mail. We write to girls and they couldn't be less interested. Who wants to write to a Marine recruit here in the states. There's no glamour to it if the Marine isn't taking a beachhead at Guadalcanal. People just don't care about men in training camps. People in this country are apathetic. It takes a war to stir them up—to get them interested in anything except their crabgrass!"

Gomer Pyle was still squinting. "Well, now see, I just don't believe you are right. I think people do care about us. Didn't the taxpayers pay for them Ping-pong tables over in the . . ."

Jim Holmes groaned. "It's no use arguing the point. People don't care about each other in general. They don't want to get involved. And they care LESS about a luckless bunch of guys who have to serve out time wearing a uniform that doesn't fit and taking orders from a knucklehead sergeant."

"Yeah, yeah, yeah," came the chorus.

Regis, alias Ray, picked it up. "We tell them we're lonely but do they do anything about it?"

"No, no, no."

Jim took his turn. "They don't think we have a right to be lonely. If we say our morale is sinking, we're accused of being soft."

"Yeah, yeah, yeah."

Ray continued with the lyrics. "They accuse us of wanting to be bottle-fed."

"Yeah, yeah, yeah."

It went on like that verse after verse with the not-so-merry chorus joining the beat. Only Gomer Pyle's earnest face reflected any sign of disagreement, but even his own open countenance was beginning to cloud. He just couldn't believe that the American people really didn't give a hoot and a holler about the boys in uniform.

But, on the other hand, he knew his fellow Marines had tried. They had put classified ads in the newspapers; they had tried to start a pen pal club; they had written to girls in each of their home towns—using the graduating high school class lists for direct mail solicitations. And not so much as a box of Brownies or a leggy picture had materialized. Not so much as a single perfumed sheet of stationery had sweetened the sharp leathery smell of the mail pouch.

Gomer Pyle just couldn't believe that people didn't care, but he had heard the mail orderly with his own ears and he had seen the fruitless returns with his own eyeballs.

It didn't seem right to Gomer Pyle. He'd always been taught that a person was supposed to love his neighbor whether his neighbor was stewing in a Marine training camp or marching off a landing craft.

Gomer entertained the argument privately, in his own mind like his Grandma Pyle had always told him to do. "Gomer," she used to say, "there's three sides to every argument: your side, their side, and the right side."

So Gomer totted up the facts. The people *did* care. But the people just weren't showing it. And if they weren't showing it, how were the Marines to know about it?

Gomer felt as sorry for his platoon buddies as he did for his old hound dog when the poor critter got the mange. He decided that talking to the platoon wasn't going to help. Talking wouldn't solve this problem any more than a hen can get a family by setting on cold storage eggs.

Gomer Pyle resolved, instead, to do something.

Had the platoon been less intent on its session of self-pity, it might have noticed Gomer taking out some paper and wetting the point of his pencil on the tip of his tongue.

Chapter Two

A FEW DAYS LATER, the Sinking Springs Community Church received the following letter:

> Dear Pastor Goins and howdy one and all,
>
> This here is Gomer Pyle talking and as you know I am a far piece from home up here training to be a Marine so I can defend you and yours if things should take a turn for the bad, which I sincerely hope they won't with all my heart.
>
> Which puts me in mind of what the boys in my platoon was saying as we were setting for a spell passing the time of day today. They allowed that civilians don't care a thing in the world about servicemen in peaceful times, which is now. They said it takes a shooting war for people in this country to want to cheer up the boys in uniform.
>
> Now, that is what they said, for a fact. I wouldn't give you a bushel of corn silks for their spirits right at the present time. I feel plumb terrible about this and I know you will feel likewise as it is simply false

that people in the land of the free and the home of the brave don't care about their fighting men who are not fighting.

But the facts of the matter are as follows: The boys in the platoon are not getting any U.S. mail and they are pretty lonesome.

I am writing because I know I can count on you folks back home and the girls in the Sunday School class to prove me out.

Therefore, I would be much obliged if you would take pen in hand and write to the enclosed names which I have put down on another page of paper.

Love, Gomer Pyle

P.S. If you don't mind, please don't dwell on the johnny grass problem. I'll explain at a later date. G.P.

Pastor Haskell Goins was not a fat man, but because his socks were always coming down and he had a chapped mouth and nose, he put one in mind of a baby. On top of it all, he had to breathe through his mouth because of a bad case of the adenoids. But he could preach up a storm. He could preach you right out of your sinful skin. He could make you feel the coals of perdition in the soles of your shoes. He could put you to thinking about fire so hard that there wasn't a female member of the Sinking Springs congregation who didn't, sometime or another during a Sunday scorcher, begin to wonder if she'd unplugged the electric iron.

But worse than the scorchers were the "for shame" sermons.

When Pastor Goins went into one of the "for shame" sermons, he could make your guilty flesh crawl.

This Sunday morning, he put aside the Bible and unfolded Gomer Pyle's letter and put it on the pulpit stand. He moved the Bible, because he always preached that nothing should be put on top of the Bible.

Then he looked out into the faces of the faithful and asked:

"Who here has mailed off a letter to Gomer Pyle since he left our number to join up with the Marine Corps?"

The flutter of the Purkey Funeral Home cardboard fans wavered and a few of the artificial roses on the ladies' flowered hats trembled a little. But nary a hand showed.

Pastor Goins went to working his chubby fingers in and out of his eyesockets, making like he wasn't seeing so good. "Hands!" he sang out. "I call for a show of hands of all them who has taken pen in hand to say hello to Gomer."

The Purkey Funeral Home fans dropped like dead birds into the laps of the multitude. But not a hand went up.

"Oh, I guess I *do* see right," Pastor Goins said in the same tone of voice he used when there were I.O.U.s in the collection plate. "I 'spect you don't recall Gomer Pyle!"

Well now, not recalling Gomer Pyle would have been one for the history books. After all, about one third of those sitting in that church were kin to Gomer in one way or another.

"I suppose," said the pastor, "that you all forgot how Gomer got the church screens?"

No went the heads and the flowered hats. No, they hadn't forgotten.

Gomer Pyle was an usher at a wedding that hot June night. And even though the incident that happened didn't happen to Gomer, it was the incident which had convinced Gomer to get screens for the windows.

The incident happened to Gomer's pal, Billy White Burnsides. Billy White was the vocalist and he could sing the strings out of your shoes.

Well, just before Billy White got up to sing "I Love You Truly," the church began to snap with those hard summer bugs which had come in through the windows—open as wide as the mouths of fools. But nobody took any notice of the hard-shelled bugs snapping away against the ceiling lights.

Then Billy White got up to sing and he got all the way through the song down to the end, where he opened his mouth real wide for the last "trooo-leee" when in flew one of them hard-shell summer bugs. Well, Billy White's eyes came out so far that he could of propped his music on them.

And everybody set forward, holding their breaths to see if Billy White was going to spit out that bug or what. There wasn't a soul born of woman but hadn't seen it fly into Billy White's mouth. Plain as day.

For a second or two, Billy White just stood there with his eyes coming out on stems. Then he tugged at his button-down collar just a tad and done the bravest thing Gomer Pyle had ever seen. He swallowed that bug. Swallowed it right down and let open his mouth to sing out the last "TROOO-LEE DEEEER!"

Gomer was impressed no end. He was so impressed that he went out single-handedly and hoed potatoes at Horace Groiner's truck farm until he made enough money for the church to have screens on the windows.

The story went through everybody's mind, of course, and by now they were all looking at the screens and thinking about Gomer Pyle. And Pastor Goins must have been satisfied that was the case because he said:

"I reckon you didn't forget Gomer and I reckon you do still care about him and all the other boys in the uniform of our country, the United States of America. I reckon them boys is wrong when they say we have got to be at WAR before anybody cares about the men in uniform." He thumped Gomer's letter with the back side of his index finger. "THAT'S WHAT IT SAYS HERE IN THIS LETTER. That it takes a war to make people show they care.

"Well, I hope to Betsy that ain't true!" The pastor's face was reddening up, and this looked like it was going to be one of his "for shame" sermons. Everybody squirmed.

Sure enough, he leaned on the pulpit the way he did when he felt a "for shame" sermon coming on. Then he began:

"My eyes ain't so good," he said. "But be that as it may, the LORD sees a sight more than I do. But I'll tell you one thing the Lord don't see. He don't see anybody in this congregation baking up a mess of cookies in their automatic electric stove to send off to Gomer Pyle.

"The Lord don't see it because it ain't taking place.

"AND I'LL TELL YOU SOMETHING ELSE THE LORD DON'T SEE. THE LORD DON'T SEE *WHY!*

"He don't see WHY because he don't see you setting in your kitchens any more shellin' up a peck of peas. He don't see you shellin' peas because He sees you taking a box of frozen peas out of your big new refrigerator and hotting them up on your big new electric range.

"The Lord has seen fit to lighten your burden, but the Lord don't see you using any of that extra time to put a pie in the oven for Gomer Pyle. The Lord has seen fit to put a sweeping machine in your living room and a tractor in your field so you won't be chained to your work ALL the time, yet He don't see you using so much as a measly minute of that time to set down and pen a letter to Gomer Pyle.

"The Lord give you television so you wouldn't even have to leave your house and go down to the Princess Theater to see a show, but the Lord don't see you turning the tee-vee off to frost a angel food cake for Gomer Pyle.

"GIVE, GIVE, GIVE. The Lord has been giving, giving, giving. And TAKE, TAKE, TAKE. You have been taking, taking, taking. The Lord has give you automatic sewing machines, but He don't see you knittin' any warm socks for Gomer Pyle.

"GIVE, GIVE, GIVE. AND TAKE, TAKE, TAKE. Oh, but we are greedy. Give to us, Lord! That's all we cry. Give us more, Lord. And give it to us NOW. We can't wait, Lord. We want, want, want.

"Don't wait for trouble to strike before You shower us with Your blessings, Lord. Don't let a body have to come down with the croup before You show us Your love, Lord! No, we couldn't stand that."

The veins came out in Pastor Goins' neck. "WELL, THEM BOYS DON'T WANT TO GO TO WAR BEFORE YOU SHOW THEM YOUR LOVE NEITHER,

PEOPLE! I say to you: 'Do unto others.' Now, bow your heads and let's pray and when the prayer is done, don't line up at the door like usual after services because I don't want to shake any hands today. "Nossir."

"I don't want to shake any hands until them hands has took up a pen and wrote to Gomer Pyle and all them in his outfit."

The Sinking Springs congregation streaked out of the church and dispersed themselves to their various kitchens. Them as still had wood-burning ranges hotted them up with an armful of kindling and shavings. Them as had automatics pushed every button in sight.

Then they plundered their larders. Out came the flour, the sugar, the shortening. Up from the root cellar came the dusty, mildew-covered jars of jams and jellies. Up came Mason jars full of pink, pickled pigs' feet. Up came the big bottles of tenderloin beef.

The cupboards spewed forth baking powder, baking soda, shredded coconut, apple, cherry and boysenberry pie fillings, walnuts and pecans. Billows of flour settled like fallout on the kitchen floors.

The inspired, shamed ladies of Sinking Springs, in one enormous surge of patriotic energy, turned out fifteen cherry, twenty-one potato, eight boysenberry and thirty-two fried apple pies. They baked eighteen devil's food with coconut frosting, thirty-two angel food with no frosting, and eight yellow with chocolate frosting cakes; and one hundred dozen sugar cookies, round and star-shaped. They fetched up six dozen jars of grape jelly, three dozen jars of strawberry jam, two dozen jars of peach preserves, eighteen quarts of pigs' feet, twelve jars of canned tenderloin. They whipped up sixty-two dozen beaten biscuits and wrapped up eight whole hickory smoked (black with pepper) country hams, wrapped up the whole kit and kaboodle and tied it with string.

Then, flapping their aprons, they dusted off the kitchen table, sat their daughters down on the rush-bottomed chairs and didn't let the girls up until each and every one of them had written to each and every one of the boys in Gomer's platoon.

The Sinking Springs post office didn't have enough air-mail stamps to go around and had to sell fives and threes.

And the parcel post . . . It took the post office four days to work out from under the parcel post.

Chapter Three

Gomer Pyle was thinking sweet thoughts, singing "Bringing in the Sheaves" and scrubbing the underside of a wash-basin in the Head when Sgt. Harold Q. Carter came up from behind and said:

"Pyle."

Gomer didn't hear the sergeant for two reasons. One was that he had just warmed up to the chorus—". . . we will come rejoicin' . . ." The other reason Gomer didn't hear was that the sergeant had spoken in a normal tone of voice. This was remedied:

"PYLE!"

Gomer, squatting, swung around on his honkers; the long-handled brush—soapy lather in its whiskers—swung with him. "Why hideee there, Sergeant Carter," Gomer said, failing to observe that his quick turn had brought the brush together with the sergeant's trousers and had left a generous helping of wet and bubbles in the region of his superior's ankles. "You give me a start there for a second," Gomer said, scrambling to his feet and beaming down on the sergeant.

Sgt. Carter had been trying his best to transform Gomer from a friendly puppy into a good leatherneck.

He controlled himself now, decided to ignore the water

seeping into his shoes, and sighed. "Pyle," he said. "Didn't I tell you to come to attention every time I speak to you?"

Gomer had a way of acting out the word "shucks." The performance involved four simultaneous gestures: a twist of his torso, a bite on his lower lip, a stamp of his right foot, and a snap of his right thumb and forefinger. He always acted out "shucks" when he was irritated with himself for forgetting something. He acted out "shucks" and then said: "You're right, you sure did tell me to come to attention, Sergeant Carter."

"Then *come to attention!*"

Gomer figured he couldn't comply neatly with the brush in his hands, so with a modified "present arms" he brought the brush up and tucked it, stalk first, under his left arm. The motion unleashed a new round of twinkling foam which found its mark just under the third button on the sergeant's tunic.

Gomer resisted the urge to wipe away his damage and stood at rigid attention.

Carbonated bubbles of anger began to rise in Sgt. Carter. "Pyle," he said. "I don't want to get angry with you."

Gomer smiled. "I don't want you to neither, Sergeant Carter, so that makes two of us."

"Pyle," said the sergeant. "I came in here to ask you a simple, friendly question."

Gomer beamed. "Well, you're sure enough my FRIEND. What can I do for you, Sergeant Carter?"

Carter cleared his throat and dusted damply at his third button. "Your hometown, Pyle, isn't that a place called Sinking Springs?"

Gomer's grin grew longer. "I hope to tell you it is!! Lord-a-mercy, is it ever purty this time of year. You ought to see it with the redbuds and the dogwoods in bloom. It's a sight for *your* sore eyes." Gomer hesitated. "Oh, now I don't mean YOUR eyes is sore. That's just a manner of speakin', that is, nothing personal meant about *your* eyes." Gomer was sadly aware that his manner of speaking was, often as not, confusing to the sergeant. Lately the recruit had been trying extra hard to communicate clearly. "See," he said, "one look at them marshmeller clouds in that blue sky would make your sore eyes feel better than a whole bucket of eyewash IF you had sore eyes."

The sergeant had heard the expression and his patience was raveling. "Pyle . . ."

"See, the town itself jest sort of nestles back of Big Bunion Ridge, that's my Uncle Muley's place—he owns all of Big Bunion."

The thought of Uncle Muley so inspired Gomer that he bounced a little and, with unerring grace, kicked over his bucket of soapy water.

However, to say he kicked it *over* was not entirely accurate. He sort of kicked it UP and over. The water reached up like a large gray arm which lost its form as it embraced the sergeant. Sgt. Carter's face turned a sort of off-rust color, the hue that home furnishing magazines were pushing for drapes that year.

Gomer was too startled to do anything.

The sergeant's uniform was host to a multitude of rivulets and foamy globules. Some of the lather took flight with the same agility as if it had been blown from a child's bubble pipe.

Neither spoke. The doused uniform clung to the drill instructor's frame, which was chunky and beginning to thicken at the waist. The sergeant was shorter than Gomer with a broader chest and short muscular arms.

And just under his crewcut and broad brow, the sergeant's face was dancing the frug. The anger, like trapped carbonation, blew the lid off his corked reserve.

"P * Y * L * E!!!!"

Sgt. Carter had come in peace to ask Gomer a simple question: a question about mail. The mail orderly had told Carter that the platoon had just received three bags of airmail letters—all from a place called Sinking Springs. The town's name had rung a bell, so Carter had decided —in all innocence and with all good will—to stroll in and ask Gomer about it.

But now he stood, after just two minutes with Gomer Pyle, reduced to a bundle of wet wash.

"That's clean dirty water, Sergeant Carter, sir," Gomer blurted. "It's all full of disinfectant and all."

Anger and his wet clothing made the sergeant's teeth chatter and his head throbbed with plans for Gomer's punishment.

Gomer gulped. "I'm sorry as I can be," he said, wilting paper towel after paper towel against the wreckage. "I reckon you are just going to have to change clothes, Sergeant Carter, sir."

"Pyle! Stand up and stop fooling with those towels and answer one simple question. Can you do that, Pyle?"

"I can sure as the dickens try," said Gomer.

"All right," said the sergeant, backing off slightly, for even though he couldn't imagine what else Gomer could do in the way of harm, he was far from convinced that the recruit had exhausted his repertoire.

Standing a good yard away from Gomer, Carter asked:

"Pyle, why is the platoon getting three large bags of mail from Sinking Springs?"

Gomer's face lit up like a klieg light. "Oh, hot diggity. I knowed it. I knowed them folks would write. Well, now, if that ain't just GRAND. I reckon that will fix up everybody a time or two. Them fellers, Sergeant Carter, they've been looking plumb peaked lately—like a calf that's off its milk. And that ain't so far-fetched neither. Them fellers has been off their feed a tad."

Just what all of this had to do with his question was far from being lucid to Carter. Bravely, the sergeant took two steps and leaned close to Gomer, and on tiptoe, put his nose near Gomer's nose and bawled:

"Just answer me why the platoon is getting three bags of mail from Sinking Springs. DO YOU READ ME?"

"Yessir, I read you loud and clear, Sergeant Carter, sir. But do you mean why THREE bags, 'cause if you do, I'm just going to have to tell you I don't have the foggiest notion why the platoon got three bags instead of two bags or four bags or one bag."

The sergeant was breathing hard. "Now Pyle, listen carefully. I don't CARE how MANY bags. Just answer in ONE

SENTENCE why you recruits are getting a lot of mail from Sinking Springs."

"Not just us recruits. I put your name down too, Sergeant Carter, so you ought to have some letters in there."

Sgt. Carter measured his words. "One sentence, Pyle. ONE sentence! Answer me in one sentence!"

Gomer shifted and lolled his head off to one side. "I can't do that, Sergeant Carter, not in one sentence, I can't. Maybe I could do it if you was to give me a paragraph."

The only reason the buttons didn't pop off the sergeant's tunic was that the fabric, being wet, stretched to accommodate the air he was pulling into his lungs.

"Pyle!"

Gomer twisted. "You know I'd do anything in the world to oblige you, Sergeant Carter, sir. I like you an awful lot and you're my friend for true. But I can't put it into one sentence, try as I might. . . ."

"All right, take a paragraph, but make it a SHORT paragraph."

Gomer heaved a sigh at his release from the binding covenant.

"Well, it's like this, Sergeant Carter sir. The fellers was out of tune, off their feed—you know, sort of mopey like. Whop-sided. I felt sorry for them. I wanted to help them in the worst way."

"Little Mary Sunshine," the sergeant growled between his shivering teeth, as he conjured up plans to avenge his wetness.

"No sir, Sergeant Carter, I didn't write to nobody by *that* name. I don't even *know* a girl by *that* name and I know a lot of girls."

A little puff of steam billowed out of Carter's wet nostrils. "GET TO THE POINT!"

Gomer bobbed his head. "So, come to find out, the reason the fellers was down and out was that they wasn't getting no mail. Oh, now, I don't mean NO mail. I just mean not MUCH mail. See, they was saying that the reason they don't get much mail is that folks don't want to write to servicemen in peacetime because they ain't no glamour in it. They said the folks don't care none for the fighting men unless they are bearing arms for real."

Gomer grinned and shrugged. "Knew they was wrong. Knew it. I sent a letter to the church back home and asked if they cared and . . ." he sighed, ". . . reckon they do."

A fly zizzed around the sergeant's head, swooping in tighter and tighter circles as it reconnoitered for a choice spot to land.

"Your church?" asked the sergeant in a small voice.

Gomer nodded. "Good folks care and most folks is good. Most folks is patriotic down deep. And when the fellers gets them letters their morale will shoot up like a thermometer in August."

"Patriotic," the sergeant whispered. "Church. Morale." The plans brewing under his wet crewcut evaporated like the bubbles on his uniform. How could he punish the recruit when such golden motives as morale and patriotism had been displayed? How could he avenge a wet uniform after Gomer had just finished reciting a good deed—a good deed involving a church?

Sgt. Carter nodded slowly, turned and walked out, a soggy and beaten man.

Chapter Four

THE LETTER READING society was in session when Gomer Pyle reached the barracks, but Gomer noticed right away that something was strange. The men were sitting in neat, orderly rows on their bunks—not a single one had hunkered down on the floor in his anxiety to rip into his mail. No one was leaning against the wall. No one was reading aloud from a cherished passage.

"Hidee, everybody," said Gomer.

"Hi, Gomer."

"Hullo, Gome."

"Yeh, Hi."

Brief greetings and some grunts and the ominous silence fell again. Gomer was puzzled, but he was often puzzled so he didn't let that bother him. "Well," he said, slapping his sides. "Isn't this here nice? Every last one of us has got mail!" He stood in the middle of the room grinning and working his neck around. "See, what did I tell you. People does care."

"Uh? Oh, uh huh."

"Sure, fine."

Fat Gorley, a pudgy boy from Ohio who still read by running his fingers under the words and pronouncing them to himself by forming the words silently, looked up and lost his place.

Fat had the countenance of a person who is perpetually startled. In fact, when Fat was really startled, nobody could tell because he couldn't look any different than when he was just looking normal.

Truth to tell, he was startled at this moment, for having spent his schooling being last in his class, he had finally come across some grammar worse than his own. He dropped his eyes back to his letter, searched for his place and started to mouth the words again.

None of the recruits knew how to tell Gomer that this gaggle of backwoods womanhood was not exactly what their hearts were yearning to yearn for. Backwoods wasn't so bad as the mental pictures stumbling across their brain pans. Any time Gomer had ever mentioned the girls back home it was either to boast about how some tomato could "whup" him at Indian "rassling" or to crow in delight at the remembered vision of some frill slopping the hogs.

It was not exactly moonlight and roses. It was more like succotash and fat back.

It was not, definitely not, the sort of southern womanhood you imagined floating across a plantation lawn. No, definitely not the kind of quail you might see in one of those big white hooped dresses. No, definitely not the sort of gumdrop who would wear a magnolia in her hair and coo: "I just love Yankee men," seduction oozing from every slow, soft syllable.

Gomer sensed a thin blue mist of gloom.

"Did somebody write to you all about johnny grass?" he asked, trying to get at the reason for the less than thunderous reception Sinking Springs was getting from his fellow recruits.

Regis, alias Ray, looked up sadly, met the eyes of the others and accepted, with his usual fatalistic attitude, the chore of being spokesman.

He was a pessimistic fellow. At twenty he had long since decided that every silver lining had its cloud. Often he said: "I used to think my ship would come in, but now I realize it was the *Andrea Doria*."

Ray was a pleasant looking, small fellow with eyes set far apart in his roundish head. In fact, if they had been any farther apart, they would have been in his ears.

It was the eyes that had caused Gomer to take an instant liking to him. Ray put teeth in one of Gomer's grandma's pet theories.

Gomer's grandma had always told him that you could tell a Republican by how close together his eyes were. "Republicans is narrow between the eyes," she said. Conversely, it followed that a Democrat was wide between the eyes. Now, Gomer had never taken up with this line of reasoning, and, as far as politics were concerned Gomer considered himself an independent. But when it had turned out that Ray, who had the most far-apart eyes Gomer had ever clapped his own glims on, was sure enough a Democrat, Gomer had been overjoyed. Despite Ray's fixation for hanging crepe, Gomer had taken a special liking for his living proof of his grandma's theory.

Ray got up and looked out of his mournful far-apart eyes and said:

"Gome, uh, these girls. Uh, they have, uh, kind of funny names and . . ."

Gomer blinked.

Regis-Ray, who had accepted Gomer's nickname for him with his usual fatalistic acceptance of things, said:

"We just haven't ever come across girls like this and . . ."

"You ain't likely to," Gomer said proudly.

Regis-Ray nodded. "But look Gome . . ." He bent down and plucked up one of the lilac perfumed envelopes. "Melody Belle Drum. What's she like?"

Gomer swung his arms happily. "She's one of the Singing Drums. Whole family sings. They sing all over—weddings, civic doings, revival meetings, high school graduations, and, twice I know of they've been on the radio." Gomer rocked back and forth. "Whole family has musical names."

Regis-Ray's rather small mouth had come open but both of his far-apart eyes were still coordinating.

"See," said Gomer, "Daddy Drum just loves music, so when his first little girl baby was born he called her Melody Belle. Then come Xylo Viola, the alto. Then Clara Nettie, soprano, Mandy Lynn and Reveille Lullaby on the harmony. Then Organ; far as I know she hasn't got a middle name to her name. Is that seven girls? No, I plumb near forgot Harmony Carol."

"Seven girls," said Regis-Ray, his far-apart eyes now woggling heavenward. "That's almost an octave."

"Oh, they have a boy, too. Daddy Drum wanted a boy in the worst way. Said to M'am Drum that they was going to keep at it until they got them a boy even if they had to collect an all-girl orchestra.'" Gomer grinned. "But next crack out of the barrel they got Hymn."

"Him?"

"Yup, Hymn."

Ray looked even more depressed than before and that was an accomplishment.

Jim Holmes, the big New York boy, decided to spell Ray. Besides he was tired of being silent. Jim had been raised in Queens by an aunt who owned a funeral home and Jim had come out of the whole thing with a desire to be loud. It was more than he could bear to be quiet for five minutes. All those years of being shusshed and told to walk slowly because his corduroy pants went "wheek-wheek-wheek" had brought him to this point in life with an almost unquenchable appetite for noise.

"Look, Gome," he boomed, stomping across the room and secretly wishing his pants made more noise. "We all owe you a vote of thanks and all, but . . ."

"Oh, now nosiree," said Gomer, holding up his right hand, palm out. "None of that. Don't you fellers get any notion you owe me anything. If you want to thank anybody, thank them folks that wrote."

The noise in Jim's big throat sank to a gurgle.

Gomer made a pushing motion with his hand. "You all just go on and enjoy them letters and don't pay no mind to being obliged. You all DESERVE them letters."

All heads wondered what they had done to deserve such letters, but no one spoke.

Gomer flapped his arms. "Lissen, I am going over to the PX for some peppermint gum. Can I git anybody anything?"

All heads shook no.

"Okey-doke," said Gomer. "Be right back."

Gomer's foot had no sooner hit the last barracks' step than the dull roar of disconsolate voices replaced the silence.

"How do we tell him that these girls turn us off?" wailed Ray.

"Oh, I dunno," said Fat Gorley. "I don't mind dumb women so much."

"Dumb? Who said anything about minding dumb?" roared Jim Holmes. "Dumb is fine. Ugly is different."

"Ugly and strong. Don't forget strong," piped Ray, "with muscles as big as New England boiled dinners."

"What are we going to do?" Jim exploded.

"Without hurting Gomer's feelings," said Fat Gorley, who was swift to go along with any mounting current.

"Listen to this gal's moniker," said another recruit. "Leafy Mae Sipe. And she has just got her driver's license . . . for the TRACTOR! Imagine what she *looks* like."

"A dog," moaned Ray. "A real beast."

Just to say something Jim Holmes said: "Well, maybe it won't hurt us to write to them."

Ray slapped his forehead in the space between his eyes. "WRITE to them! And have them on our necks? WRITE to them! And build up their hopes!"

Jim ran his hand down the back of his head, which was flat because his aunt had been too busy in the coffin room to turn him over when he was a baby. "Gomer thinks he's done us a real service."

"Yeah," said Fat Gorley, looking surprised and trying his best to fight down an urge to write to these dogs in secret.

A rumble of dejection was punctured by Jim. "I vote we just come right out and level with Gomer."

"Shuush," said Fat Gorley, who had just seen Gomer approaching.

Jim, who had had enough of being shusshed in the funeral home, whirled around. "Don't shussh ME, Gorley! Don't you *ever* shuush me or I'll knock your teeth down your throat."

Fat had protruding teeth and half wished Jim *would* knock them down his throat and rid him of them. But Gomer was already in the barracks.

"I knew it," Gomer said. "You all are fighting over them girls. Already!" He beamed joyously and rocked his head from side to side. "Fighting already over them girls."

"Well, not exactly . . ." Ray began.

"Nothin' to be ashamed of," Gomer cut in. "That's just healthy. But I'll let you all in on a secret. They's enough girls in Sinking Springs to go around twice and then some. Folks in Sinking Springs has a real green thumb when it comes to girls. Yessir, we got more girls than we know what to do with."

No one felt like arguing that.

Gomer loped to his bunk and, feeding stalk after stalk of gum into his toothsome face, began to open his own mail.

Gomer had been taught by his grandma to linger over

anything good, so his letter reading took his off-duty time for the rest of the day and ran well into the night.

All gentle attempts by the men to tell Gomer that they weren't interested in the brand of women so prolifically produced in his hometown met with dismal failure. The more the attempts, the more Gomer interpreted the words and actions of his fellows as those of unbridled delight. Each effort made by the recruits to tell Gomer their true feelings got turned back on them.

That night before lights-out, Gomer lay reading, slapping his thigh over this or that and punctuating his slappings with "you-don't-mean-its."

Little snatches of news sprinkled his monologue. It emerged that his Uncle Muley was building a swimming pool with his own hands; that a big corn roast was coming up; that Billy White Burnsides, who had so awed Gomer with his bug-swallowing feat, had given up singing for the summer to play the part of an Indian in an outdoor drama; and that the town had a new firetruck with a 97 foot ladder that was some 37 feet higher than any building in town.

"You don't mean it," Gomer said. "Lissen to this." He cleared his throat and read: "Old Horace Groiner's tractor broke the other day and as he was hauling it over to Pewkey's Garage, it busted free and went lickety-split for the flagpole on the courthouse lawn. . . .

"This means," Gomer read, pausing to turn the page, "that we don't have a flagpole on the football field no more." He shook his head at the shame of it.

Ray twisted irritably. "Now why is that? Why if the flagpole at the courthouse . . .?"

Gomer smiled up at him. "I ain't got that far, but I reckon the tractor must of smushed the flagpole on the courthouse lawn."

Ray groaned. "On the *courthouse* lawn, Gome. Not in the football field. You said they didn't have a flagpole in the football field."

"I didn't say," said Gomer, "I read. But it's easy as pie to understand THAT. Flagpole on the courthouse lawn is far and away more important than the flagpole on the football field, important as *that* is. And if the flagpole on the courthouse lawn got smushed it would be the most natural thing in the world to move the flagpole on the football field over to the courthouse lawn."

Ray felt a headache starting up in his temples.

"Anyway," Gomer said, "I didn't get that far." He cleared his throat again and continued: "Well sir, that tractor went streaking for that flagpole and wrangled into it and knocked it flatter than a bride's first angel food cake." Gomer angled out of his bunk to look up at Ray, who had the bunk over him. "See?"

Ray moaned softly. But Gomer read on.

"Mrs. Groiner was steering the tractor when the event took place and was throwed free only to land head first against the curbing." Gomer shuddered but read on quickly. "However, the Lord had seen to it that she was to put up her hair in them spongy-type hair curlers just minutes before they left the house. So, when her head hit the curb, them spongy curlers just sort of bounced. Doctor said they had saved her life. They was all ground down, like, and full of cinders. But she didn't have a scratch." Gomer sighed and piped up to Ray. "You ever hear the like?"

Since Ray didn't answer, Gomer continued with the letter. "Thing about it was that Mrs. Groiner had just that day bought them hair curlers at a benefit for the church. So, if you don't see the Lord's hand in that, you are blind. However, we don't have no flagpole at the football field as a sad, regretful result."

The really big news, so far as Gomer was concerned, however, came two letters later. That was that his best friend (aside from Billy White Burnsides) had taken to courting a girl. Gomer's best friend, outside of Billy White, was a chap by the name of Menlo Acuff. But the distressing part of the news was that the girl wasn't a LOCAL girl.

Gomer couldn't get over that. His fellow recruits had no trouble getting over it. Gomer couldn't imagine it. His fellow recruits had no problem imagining it. Gomer's fellow recruits secretly congratulated Menlo Acuff on his standards.

Then, just before lights out, Gomer reached for the last item in his pile of mail. It was a brown envelope and it disgorged a thirty-six inch photograph, folded in three places to accommodate it to its envelope.

"Lord, just lookie at Menlo," Gomer gasped.

Gomer sat up in his bunk and held the picture out from him. He was holding the picture horizontally, however, and the recruits across the room saw only the back side, a white expanse, thirty-six inches long and about six inches high.

Had he held it vertically, it might have indicated that Menlo Acuff was a very long, skinny, thin fellow. But horizontally, Menlo promised to be at least six times as broad as he was long.

"Why, if that ain't the worst picture Menlo ever had taken," Gomer said.

Ray, in the bunk over Gomer, groaned and came off his pillow. In one motion, he flipped himself to the edge of his bunk and popped his torso out and down to take a look at this Menlo.

One quick gander at the photograph and Ray's far-apart eyebrows stood at attention. Then, in a thrashing of short arms and legs, Ray, scrabbling for sheet, pillow, mattress—anything—anything to cling to—came flapping down in a disordered cloud of bedclothes at Gomer's feet.

Ray, who ordinarily would have adored such an excuse to opine his bad luck or to exhibit his ill-fortuned bruises, brushed aside all of these opportunities and fought free from his tangle of sheets in time to snap the picture out of Gomer's hands before the other recruits converged on it.

Menlo was probably in the picture, though no one took note of him. Vaguely they might have realized that a man was standing in the middle of the photograph, eyes closed and holding a sign which said "YOUNG WOMEN'S BIBLE CLASS, SINKING SPRINGS, MENLO ACUFF TEACHER."

But stretched out to the left of him and stretched out to the right of him for thirty-six glorious inches were the most agonizingly luscious females ever to assemble before one photographer's lens in the history of emulsion.

Fat Gorley looked startled, as usual. But so did every other recruit—to the man.

And all that night, by match light, twinkling like fireflies, the men crept over to gander once more and once again, at the most adorable pen pals any boy could want.

Chapter Five

EARLY THAT NEXT morning, Sgt. Harold Q. Carter sat, chin in hand, at his gray-green metal desk.

Before him, unopened, were nine perfumed letters. Behind him were thirty-two years of abject defeat in his relentless pursuit of the female of his species. Actually, he was thirty-two years old but he didn't count the first three years although he could have, for at two and a half he had clapped his sticky baby hands on a sun-suited cutie only to be beaned by her sand bucket.

The pattern had not altered appreciably in the thirty-two and a half years which had followed.

It was not that he wasn't attractive. He was certainly a cut above a lot of the bruisers who had no trouble getting dates.

The trouble was a combination of things. Timing, the breaks, the right moment, the right girl, the right situation. He supposed you could call it luck, although Sgt. Carter was not the kind of fatalistic animal who liked to brood or blame chance for his or anyone else's mishaps. Yet in his forays into the world as a Casanova, things were slightly off register, out of sync and smacking of the qualities of an echo or a stutter.

At the age of eight, when he had attempted to dunk, lovingly, a pigtail into an inkwell, the well was dry. At twelve, he chose as the recipient of his first mouth-to-mouth contact, the bubble gum champion of Grand Trees Grade School. Sneaking up behind her, he did not see that she was in the birth throes of a bubble to put a dirigible to shame.

At fifteen, he picked the prettiest, blue-eyest be-dimplest darling in English and his homeroom, and snitching her *Adventures in American Literature,* he scrawled in indelible ink on its flyleaf: "I love you with heart and soul, Harold." She threw the book at him because it was one she had borrowed from her steady beau, who was a tackle on the football team and whom Harold Carter would never forget.

At sixteen, Harold Quinten Carter was gunshy. Rather, he was sand pail, inkwell, bubble gum, and book-shy. But the same qualities which were to make him a good Marine forced him to try again.

At twenty-one, in San Francisco, Carter had just slipped his arm around a curvacious beauty when an earth tremor shook her out of his reach and deposited her neatly into the arms of an ensign.

At twenty-five, in Chicago, he had made a heavy date with a tantalizing redhead when all the Transportation Employees, Local 369, went on strike bringing the city to a halt and sucking in the taxis in sympathy. He never got to her.

At thirty, on leave in Dubuque, Iowa, he lined up a rowboat to court a corn farmer's silken-haired daughter. That was the day the Mississippi River flooded and hit its highest crest in fifty years.

Sgt. Harold Q. Carter sighed, took his chin out of his palm, reached across his gray-green metal desk, plucked up the nine perfumed letters, which were eight more than he had ever received in one crop from girls before, and dropped them gingerly into his wastebasket.

As if to put an exclamation point on it, his screen-door spanked with a "spak" and Fat Gorley shambled in with brush and dusters to clean the tops of things, polish the sergeant's boots and empty all waste receptacles.

Fat stood at attention, or what passed as attention with

Fat. There were so many drooping parts of Fat Gorley that only about 72 per cent of him was at attention at any given time. Sgt. Carter was pleased to have problems like slapping Fat into shape. It took his mind off the gentler gender.

Fat's startled countenance jiggled Sgt. Carter's mind into action. "Where's Pyle?" he growled. It was Gomer's day to mop the floor and clean the undersides of things. Sgt. Carter looked at his watch and repeated, "Where's Pyle?"

"Barracks, I guess," Fat muttered.

"Doesn't he know he's late!" barked the sergeant as he began to watch the second hand on his timepiece.

"I dunno," said Fat.

Punctuality was not one of Gomer's attributes and patience was not one of Carter's.

Twisting irritably, Sgt. Carter glowered at the second hand and gave it three more full turns before he slammed out of his quarters and baroomed over to the barracks.

Once he darkened that door, the recruits scattered like wildly-flung confetti, exposing the vortex of their attention: Gomer Pyle and the thirty-six inch picture.

"PYLE! On your feet and at ATTENTION!"

Gomer dropped the picture, cracked his head on the overhead bunk and flew to attention so fast it put a crick in his neck.

Momentarily Carter held his distance, hesitating to come too close to Gomer for fear of fates known or unknown to him. However, with no water bucket in view, the sergeant stepped forward, pressed his nose to within smelling distance of Gomer's toothpaste and bawled:

"PYLE. YOU ARE SEVEN MINUTES LATE!"

Gomer, still at attention, and hurting to beat the band from the knock on his head and the crick in his neck, moved only his mouth. First he formed it into an "O" and then he said:

"Well, I swanney, Sgt. Carter, sir. Time just got away from me, is all I can say. I'm as guilty as the day I was born. Guiltier. Guilty as a fox in a hen-house."

"You can say that again."

"I'm as guilty as . . ."

"All right, STOP IT, Pyle."

"Yessir," said Gomer. "But I AM sorry."

"Sorry is the word for you, Pyle. The perfect, exact, precise and ACCURATE word for YOU!"

Gomer smiled in admiration. "You sure do have a way of putting things, Sergeant Carter, sir. You sure express yourself well. I sure wish I could express myself with just half the . . ."

"PYLE!"

"Yessir."

"Pyle, you are tardy and *not* punctual."

Gomer nodded solemnly. "I know it, Sergeant Carter. That's one of my worst failings, and I sure appreciate you bringing it to my attention. I'd appreciate it even MORE if you'd keep after me about it. I need to get broke of the habit and . . ."

"Pyle," sputtered the sergeant. "You have NO concept of time."

"I know it, Sergeant Carter. You keep on reminding me of that and we'll lick it yet, sir. The two of us working together on it."

Carter bit his lip until he almost brought blood. "All right, at ease, Pyle." Gomer stood at ease. Carter stepped back and surveyed the recruit. "I said at ease, Pyle."

Gomer smiled stiffly. "Oh, I AM at ease, Sergeant Carter. It's just that I have a crick in my neck and I just don't LOOK like I'm at ease. See, my arms is swinging free."

Carter expelled a small puff of wind. "All right, Pyle. Just explain why you were late."

Gomer smiled. "I just got to . . . got to . . . to fooling around, I guess. Time sneaked out like a thief in the night." Actually, his lateness had been mostly the fault of the other recruits who had pinned him down and extracted identification and details on each of the lovely doves in the thirty-six inch span of that fantastic photograph. Ray had taken a nose dive for Leafy Mae Sipe and had enlisted Gomer's help in composing his first letter to her.

"Fooling around?" snapped Carter.

"Yessir. Monkeying around. I wish you'd really get after me about that Sergeant Carter, 'cause my Uncle Muley used to complain to me about it and . . ."

Sgt. Carter raised himself on tiptoe: "What were you fooling around with, Pyle?"

Gomer stooped, keeping his neck and torso rigid while he picked up the photograph. "This, Sergeant Carter. It's a picture."

At first, Sgt. Carter only saw the length of it. It was roughly the length and height of photographs he had come across in his attic as a child—photographs of World War I American Legion Posts.

Sgt. Carter jerked the photograph from Gomer, and still glowering into the recruit's eye teeth, he asked: "What is this, anyway, Pyle?"

Gomer smiled nervously. "Just a picture. Them girls that wrote to all of us. Didn't you get no letters, Sergeant Carter?"

Sgt. Carter didn't answer because his eyes were now on the photograph and what registered against his retinas was causing every nerve cell in his brain to fire. The hope of female conquest, until now fluttering faintly in his breast, began to flop like an imprisoned wild goose, beating its wings against his rib cage.

His first thought was of the unopened letters in his wastebasket. His second, third, and fourth thoughts were of the tiny, sweet-faced brunette who was fifth from the end on the right, and with his finger on her, Carter stuttered: "W-who is sh-she?"

"Why that's Xylo Viola Drum," sang Gomer. "She sings. We all got letters from the Drum girls."

Carter remembered the name on one of the unopened letters in his wastebasket. He relinquished the picture, and spinning on the balls of his feet, swung out of the barracks.

Fat Gorley, when you weren't standing over him, usually took more than twice the normal time to execute his chores. He always shined the sergeant's boots first, then he emptied the wastebaskets.

It was well past the time he should have had the baskets empty, but with luck . . . Sgt. Carter doubled his pace.

And sure enough, Fat was just bending to pick up the wastebasket when the sergeant barrelled through the door.

Sgt. Carter was not one to believe in omens, but as he salvaged the nine letters—one of them from Xylo Viola Drum—the thought ticked in his head that his timing, for once, had been right on the money.

Chapter Six

THE U. S. POST OFFICE DEPARTMENT has a long and illustrious history. It is the branch of government set up for the purpose of carrying and delivering letters, papers and other matter that can be mailed. Today, there are about 41,000 post offices throughout the U. S. It is one of the largest business organizations in the world. In one year it does a gross business of close to three billion dollars.

The records of the General Assembly of Massachusetts chronicle, in 1639, what may have been the first post office in North America. It was in that year that the house of a certain Richard Fairbanks was made a depository "for all letters which are brought from beyond the seas or are to be sent thither. . . ."

In 1659, a postal service was established in Virginia. In 1672, a monthly postal service was put into operation between New York and Boston. In 1691, an inter-colonial post service was begun by a private individual. In 1706, the British took over this enterprise and made it a branch of the general post office in London.

In 1792, the U. S. government established a U. S. Post

Office Department. In 1847, the adhesive postage stamp came into use. In 1863 free city-delivery began. In 1864, railway mail service was initiated. In 1897, free rural-delivery started.

In 1913, the parcel-post system went into operation. And in 1965, parcel post underwent one of the unusual runs in its 52-year history. It began when the packages from Sinking Springs began to flush into the system of this old and established branch of government.

Any parcel, because it is bulky, odd-sized, and wrapped according to the many odd versions of what the senders consider proper wrapping, causes extra effort on the part of the more than 500,000 employees of the U. S. Post Office.

And "the parcels" from Sinking Springs was another matter altogether. Much of it was wrapped in crumpled brown paper and tied with a variety of different colored string—the mark of string savers, of which Sinking Springs has a goodly number. However, it was wrapped passably enough to withstand its brief encounter with the postal service. Besides, *that* was not what made it stand out from the usual run of parcel post.

What really set it apart were the messages, admonitions, reminders, and sharp commands written on the outside of the packages and directed both to the recipients and to anyone who would handle it along the way.

Postal employees had the eerie feeling that the ladies of Sinking Springs were standing over their shoulders, breathing down their necks and watching their every move. "Postal worker!" said the warning on the outside of one parcel. "This is my own special pickled tongue. Handle it like you would handle your own mother's tongue."

Another warned one and all:

"Keep Right Side Up!

The Berry Juice Didn't Set."

When they were not being admonished and sharped at by the senders of these parcels, the postal people were merely fascinated by the addendum scrawled on the crumpled brown paper.

"FRAGILE. Raisin Pie.

If they walk, they's not raisins. Ha."

At Gomer's base, the branch post office had become aware of the Sinking Springs postmark when the airmail letters had arrived. Because the Marines in the camp post office were no less anxious for extra work than any of the billions of other human beings on this earth, they took careful note of this source of their extra toil.

And when the packages began to arrive, the men were even more dismayed, and for several reasons. The extra work was the first item, naturally. That was also the second item. The third item was that, in addition to being sharped at by their superiors, the men in the camp P.O. were now being snapped at by the mail itself. ("DON'T DARE TO SHAKE THIS.")

The fourth item, and the one which concerned them least, was that the Marine Corps, while it does not *discourage* the receipt of parcels by its men, does not encourage it either.

This, of course, was the problem of the men getting the parcels and their drill instructor. The postal workers, however, hoping to diminish their own chores, brought this fact to the attention of the mail orderly, who was only too happy to bring it to the attention of the drill instructor, who was Sgt. Carter.

It was each drill instructor's responsibility as to where the men could store their goodies, just how much they were allowed to keep in the barracks and so on.

But Carter, when approached, was strangely glassy-eyed and preoccupied. And the influx, while making extra work, was not really all that heavy. Yet.

Thus did the fruits of the Sinking Springs kitchens begin to arrive at Gomer's camp. The mail, which was already cause for quickened heartbeats and higher blood pressure, what with the budding of assorted paper romances between the men and the Sinking Springs girls, now began to appeal to the stomachs as well.

At first, it came in driblets. A raisin pie here and a sweet potato pie there. Fat Gorley's protruding teeth sank with glee into the divinity candy made with pure milk from TB-tested cows by Miss Mae Pearl Acuff, Menlo's aunt and choir leader, a lady as pure as her product.

Fat Gorley ate one piece, looked startled, ate another, looked more startled—if that was possible—and then just settled down in startled joy and added to his fatty tissue.

Ray, who was finding it tough to find anything to brood about, filled his face with devil's food cake and gazed moonfully at the image of Leafy Mae Sipe on the thirty-six inch picture.

On the second day, Sgt. Carter got some oatmeal cookies in shapes that looked vaguely familiar to him. The cookies came from Xylo Viola Drum and there was something reverent about the way he handled the enclosed note which said: "I hope you enjoy eating these guitars."

The smiling image of Xylo Viola was now visited three times daily by the sergeant. Xylo Viola was tiny, with birdlike bones—sure to be shorter than the sergeant. Her bones, however, were graced with some of the most well-arranged, curvaceous flesh Carter had ever seen. She had black hair and large brown bovine eyes. From her letters, she was almost certainly not as smart as the sergeant, and that pleased him. He liked the fact that she could sing; he enjoyed music. And she seemed to be interested in him, an item that made him glassy-eyed and preoccupied.

About thirty minutes before the mail arrived each morning, every stomach in the platoon began to growl while salivary glands logged overtime.

In addition, hearts began to thump. And in still further addition, envy began to ripple throughout the base.

On the third day, the ripple of envy grew into a roar of jealousy. For, in addition to pickled calf's tongue and canned tenderloin, came thick ropes of sausages, preserved spareribs, pickled pigs' feet, homemade cheese, whole smoked hams, tins of fried chicken, boxes of beaten biscuits, loaves of homemade sandwich meat, tempting jars of pickled baby corn and the usual helping of cookies, candy, pie and cake.

Gomer Pyle received a rhubarb pie from his Cousin Marthie who had probably bought the crust makings out of her savings from the collection plate on Sundays, an angel food cake from his Aunt Beulah, and three dozen Brownies from his grandma.

And it was only the beginning.

Gomer's platoon gained a collective seventy-eight pounds.

And it kept coming.

More cookies from Xylo Viola. Banjo cookies.

Golden butter drops from the Sunshine Ladies Sewing Circle.

Pecan pie from Leafy Mae Sipe.

Marble cake . . . taffy candy . . . (imitation) rum-balls . . . coconut drops . . . cherry tarts . . .

Smoked ham, fried chicken, canned tenderloin.

Pickles.

Homemade pretzels.

"Why," said Marine Gomer Pyle, "they's enough food here to feed an army."

And still it came. And came.

It took only hours for the recruits to write home telling of this wondrous repast which had been sent forth from the aromatic kitchens of Sinking Springs. So, naturally, their own mamas, shamed by this display, scurried around their own less aromatic kitchens in Ohio, and Massachusetts, and Pennsylvania, and came forth with:

Apple strudel . . . Philadelphia scrapple . . . slabs of brisket . . . pepperoni . . . salami . . . jelly roll . . . nut bread . . . tomato pickles . . . kosher dills . . . pastrami. . . .

Poppy seed rings.

Fudge.

Artichoke hearts.

Smoked oysters.

(Real) Rum-balls.

Gomer's platoon put another burden on the scales.

Then, as it might be imagined, this news fed back to Sinking Springs, and the ladies there and their mouth-watering daughters rose to battle, and increased their offensive.

And there came to pass:

More cake. More pie. Fried pig-skins. More tenderloin. More ham. More guitar cookies.

More banjo cookies. More, and more, and more.

Sinking Springs had only begun to fight. Those ladies sponsored a Gomer Pyle Bake Sale. It netted $99.23, all of which went to buy toothpaste, shaving cream, after-shave lotion, and pocket knives.

Socks were knitted.

A "Gomer Pyle Sociable" engineered by Leafy Mae Sipe and held by the church, featured the Singing Drums and all you could eat for 99 cents. Leafy Mae was a tall, svelte redhead who had her big blue eyes on Ray's wide-apart ones.

That "do" cleared $63.19, all of which went toward combs, brushes, nail clippers, personalized toe clippers, hair tonic and genuine plastic billfolds.

But the mamas of the recruits were not finished either. They wrote to relatives in Wisconsin, Illinois, Virginia, and Florida.

From Wisconsin came cheese.

From Illinois came corned beef.

From Virginia came crates of apples.

From Florida came crates of oranges . . . crates of white grapefruit . . . crates of pink grapefruit.

At this point in the good-will skirmishes, Gomer's platoon was literally about to be killed with kindness. Things were so good, they were bad.

Close order drill wasn't as close or as orderly as it had been in the pre-mail days. Bayonet competition with the other platoons found Sgt. Carter's platoon dragging up the rear. His men oozed over the obstacle course like molasses. Their bellies got in the way at judo training.

"Why," chortled Gomer Pyle, "we are getting too big for our britches."

Sgt. Harold Q. Carter, himself overfed, brayed and coaxed and flailed his arms, but he neither brayed nor coaxed nor flailed his arms with his old vinegar.

If he bounced around too much, Xylo Viola's piano-string taffy gave him heartburn.

Storage space also was becoming a critical problem.

The accumulation of non-perishable foods had already overflowed their lockers. Regularly now, the platoon shared some of its cakes and cookies—things it couldn't store—with the other, jealous platoons. The other platoons, about to get their own fill, grew less and less jealous.

Still the salamis, the oranges, the grapefruits, the hams, and the jars and jars and jars of things kept arriving. This was to say nothing of all the toothpaste, shaving cream and toenail clippers that grew into mountains.

It was becoming more and more difficult to get through a routine inspection without a tube of shaving cream popping out of an unhinged locker.

Sgt. Carter, who brushed after every musical cookie he received from Xylo Viola, began to wax more and more gloomy about the shape of the platoon. That he was brushing with toothpaste supplied (albeit indirectly) by Xylo Viola did little to console him at this juncture.

Marine training, he reminded himself, promises to produce a physically and mentally alert man, who will fit into the pattern of a military organization which has become highly respected throughout the world. Carter's men were beginning to get physically flabby, mentally sluggish, and not even the sort of men who would fit into the pattern of a hard-driving Cub Scout troop.

Yet, he was hard put to resist the flood of goodies himself. His daily correspondence—sometimes twice a day—with Xylo Viola had grown quite serious and it was reducing him to a pulp. Besides, he couldn't think of any way to stem the tide. He didn't want to think of any way. But Sgt. Carter had his spasms of fear and remorse, and these joggled at his conscience. Mostly however, his fancy carried him on clouds to just beneath a southern moon where magnolia blossoms filled his nostrils and Xylo Viola filled his eyes and ears.

So his men stumbled through survival trials, blundered through M-14 practice, lost at push-ball, and stretched the seams of their Marine issue trousers.

Then with a clap of thunder, word came that threatened

to shatter the happy, moon-eyed, rotund, lethargic bliss of Sgt. Carter's platoon.

The inspector general's team picked this time to make its visit. With its customary last minute warning, it announced that it, led by Brig. Gen. Kenneth A. Cusps, would be on base only 72 hours hence.

Chapter Seven

"I DO BELIEVE," said Gomer's Aunt Beulah to Gomer's Uncle Muley, "that it is fixing to weather."

"You are Koo-Koo," he replied without looking up.

She stood looking down at her lawfully wedded who was, so he claimed anyway, building a swimming pool in the backyard. Their backyard was the entire top of Big Bunion Ridge which looked out over the green valley that held Sinking Springs in its palm. You could see three states if you stood on the hen house at the far end of the property. You had to stand on the hen house to see, otherwise the tall blue spruce blocked the view. Gomer's Uncle Muley didn't put much stock in that view, however, because there was no way of telling where one state left off and another began.

The view that really set him off was the one just under his nose, for just below his property and, slanting downward, all the way to Highway 66 (the main road leading into Sinking Springs and the only road on the south end) was a rag-taggle eye-sore of crumbling walls, mouldering shacks and rusty machinery.

The old Pugh place, which Uncle Muley called the old "pew" place, hung by its claws to the mountain side. Long since abandoned, and many years haunted, the old ancestral home rattled ominously in a good wind storm, its broken windows grinning like a toothless hag.

Around it in varying stages of decay were outbuildings, all at a slant, but stubbornly rooted as if growing out of the mountain: wheels, tin cans, the bones of two old trucks, a collapsed chicken house, a listing cowbarn, and a large concrete milk house. The milk house, in which a variety of reptiles now resided, was covered with moss and could hardly be seen. The remainder of the place was not so blessed.

And none of the ramshackle structures were as bad as the litter. Litter begets litter, and if people see a mess, they can't seem to stand it unless they can add to it. So, bit by bit, over the years, discarded beer cans, bedsprings, listing baby carriages, mouldy old one-legged sofas, bent fenders and bald tires joined the array.

Uncle Muley had been after the county authorities for some time, well, actually for twenty-nine years, to demolish the place and clean up the mountain side. But clearance and renewal is not a specialty in the South. Besides, getting up that mountain and carting that stuff away over the narrow, spiny roads was somehing else again.

Uncle Muley called the road up to his place "Corkscrew Avenue" and getting up that thing with a bulldozer and a headache-ball would have been a feat in itself. Even getting up it with dump trucks to haul out some of the rubbish was more than the county budget could afford. Each year, the county court appropriated for it and then, each year, a spring flood or the pot holes would eat up the appropriation and each year Uncle Muley was left with only a promise. Had he not been so stubborn, Uncle Muley would have abandoned hope when the county failed to clear it up the year of the Civil War Centennial. But he clung to hope.

In the meantime, to overcome some of the ugliness he saw when he sat in his backyard, Uncle Muley decided to build himself a swimming pool. Now, none of these fancy know-it-all scalpers were going to leech on Uncle Muley, no sir. He would build his pool with his own hands and at his own speed. Maybe his lovely grounds and pretty pool would finally shame the county into action. He doubted that, but at least it would be pretty where he lived and would counteract some of the shambling disarray on the mountain.

Gomer's Aunt Beulah made a little clucking sound—a sign that she wanted attention. Failing to get it, she said:

"Well, maybe it won't weather after all. I thought I smelled me a blow coming up."

Uncle Muley looked up from his enormous hole and squinted at the flawless, porcelain sky. "A blow. Naw. It ain't going to weather."

"I don't think so, neither," said Aunt Beulah. "And ain't *that* a blessing."

Uncle Muley put his trowel on a stack of concrete blocks and turned around to face her. He had to look at her against the sun and he squinted painfully. "Why haven't you took the rollers out of your hair? It is eleven o'clock in the morning."

"You just mind to your knitting, Mister," she said standing over him like a paper cutout silhouette. "It is none of your never mind why I have the rollers in my hair at eleven a.m. in the morning. *How-some-ever,* a body *would* think that you might know what day this is."

Uncle Muley expectorated. It was not their anniversary because that was day before yesterday. It was not his dearly beloved's birthday because that was at hog-slaughter time. It was not his own birthday because if it had been his own birthday she would have had the rollers out of her hair before seven o'clock in the morning.

"I 'spect," said Uncle Muley as he scooped up another trowelful of cement, "that you are going to stand up there and try to make me guess at what day it is."

Aunt Beulah put her hands on her hips. "Well, if you would put your mind to something besides that swimming hole, you might *know* what day it is."

Uncle Muley spanked his hat down on the stack of concrete blocks. "Put my mind on something *else!* Why, the way you talk, sounds like I don't go out and work and slave to earn your bread by the sweat of my brow."

"Well, they is more to life than running a business and building a swimming hole."

Uncle Muley slapped some more dust out of his hat. "Now how in-the-tarnation-much-time have I spent on this here pool lately? Mostly, I have been down to that store earning money so as to provide you with every darned, new-fangled household doo-dad in kingdom come."

"Money," said Gomer's Aunt Beulah, "ain't everything."

"Money," said Gomer's Uncle Muley, "is its own reward."

"They's other things in life."

"The best things in life is expensive."

"When was the last time you took me out sociable?"

"Oh, get on gone, Missus."

"No, now just think, Mister. When was the last time you and me went out sociable?"

Uncle Muley expectorated again.

"Mister, don't you get cantankerous with me. Now, you tell me when was the last time . . ."

"All right, dang it. The last time I stepped out with you was for the ramp festival."

Aunt Beulah smiled. "And how long ago was that?"

Uncle Muley slathered another trowelful of cement on the concrete blocks and pursed his lips. "Oh, going on a year ago."

Aunt Beulah tapped her foot. "Which means?"

Which meant that it was ramp festival time again.

"Today?"

"The same," said Aunt Beulah as she held out her strong right arm to help her mate scramble out of his listing concrete block monstrosity.

"Ain't it a blessing that we have got a day like this for a ramp festival," she said as they marched into the house. "I drawn you a bath."

While he was tubbing, Aunt Beulah sang in the news that the Singing Drums had a few new tricks up their sleeves for today's program.

"A old dog like me don't like new tricks," grumped Gomer's Uncle Muley.

"Well, for myself, I'm in a dither to see what they have thought up now."

"Bull," said Uncle Muley from his tepid tub. "I like the old songs best. Why don't they just stick to the old favorites."

"You sound to me like you need a good dose of the salts."

Aunt Beulah was taking out her rollers. She did this carefully so as not to disturb the curls they had made. Aunt Beulah did not see any sense in putting up your hair if you were going to comb through it and get it uncurly again. She gently patted the rows of stiff knockwursts, turning her head to survey her handiwork. Since she had only a few meager strands of hair to begin with, clumping the strands together into a scant half-dozen knockwurst curls left ample space for her white scalp to show through.

Uncle Muley began to wash under his arm pits and let the water out of the tub.

"Did you wash your ears, Mister?"

"Yes, but if you don't leave off pestering me, I'll wish I hadn't of."

"And did you wash out your eyes?"

"No, they are still in my head. Ha. Ha."

As Uncle Muley was pulling on his Sunday-go-to-meeting trousers, Aunt Beulah said:

"You know, I think that Xylo Viola Drum has took a shine to that non-commitment officer."

"Non-commissioned, Missus."

"Don't be so picky. You know well-enough what I mean. Anyway, don't you think so?"

"Think what?"

"That Xylo Viola has took a shine to that . . ." she skipped over the non-com part and went on ". . . officer in Gomer's pontoon."

"PLAN-toon," said Uncle Muley, shaking at his head to unscramble it. "Plateau . . . panton . . . poon . . . PLATOON dang it. Lord, Missus you got me so mixed up in my head that I don't know whether I am going or coming."

"At this here moment, you are going," said Aunt Beulah, clapping his good straw on his head and hustling him out the door, "to the 63rd Annual Cawkey County Ramp Festival."

When they arrived, Uncle Muley parked by the first aid station where it said "Emergency Parking Only." Uncle Muley considered it an emergency that he couldn't find any other place to park.

As he and Aunt Beulah struck out across the grass they did not make very good time because Aunt Beulah stopped every whipstitch to pass the time of day.

Willis Hoyt had a risin' on the back of his neck and Aunt Beulah had to take a close look at that.

Roy Goodpasture's wife was going on about how tight the young boys was wearing their pants these days. Roy turned to Uncle Muley. "How's business?"

"Tollable."

"You ain't shut down in a good while."

"I'll be going out of business soon."

"That's good," said Roy.

Uncle Muley was in the going-out-of-business business. He was not very good at running stores but he was a whiz at closing them down. He had been going out of business for the last thirty-one years. He had started by going out of the dry goods business. That was so lucrative that he went out of the boot-and-work-shoe business. Then he went out of the housedress and overall business. Then the hardware business. Now he was about to go out of the automotive supply business.

Uncle Muley's close-outs were a seven-state attraction and despite his sign which proclaimed LAST FOUR DAYS, they lasted months, sometimes ran to two years.

His window itself was a sight to see.

"PRICES SLASHED TO THE BONE."

"MY LOSS IS YOUR GAIN."

"IT'S LIKE STEALING ONLY IT'S LEGAL."

"I'M WHIPPED. COME IN AND GET THE BEST OF ME."

"ONE FRIED CHICKEN LEG WITH EVERY $10 PURCHASE."

"KICK ME WHILE I'M DOWN."

"LOST MY SHIRT. EVERYTHING GOES."

"SELLING OUT TO THE BARE WALLS AND MAKE ME A OFFER ON THE WALLS."

"VALUABLE DOOR PRIZES EACH DAY."

"SEEING IS BELIEVING. SO COME SEE. YOU WON'T BELIEVE."

"FREE TAIL PIPES EVERY OTHER WEDNESDAY."

"I'VE HAD IT. COME AND GET IT."

"FREE WRAPPING PAPER AND STRING WITH EVERY PURCHASE NO MATTER HOW LARGE NOR SMALL."

Everybody looked forward to those sales. It was not just the bargains, of which there were plenty. It was also the entertainment. You never knew what Uncle Muley would do next. Sometimes he would leap onto the counter and start to auction stuff off. Sometimes, he'd just pitch an armload of stuff up in the air and yell to the folks that whatever didn't fall back onto the counters was free.

For months it went that way even though the sign now said POSITIVELY LAST FOUR DAYS. On it would go until even the sign ABSOLUTELY LAST FOUR DAYS had gathered fly specks.

Uncle Muley kept his stock fresh by buying up fire sale goods, so no matter how much folks bought the walls never seemed to get bare.

Folks were glad of that. Uncle Muley's closings were far and away to be desired over anybody's openings.

Aunt Beulah pulled on him. Off they went again over the grass, but it took her thirty more minutes of talking to get where the Purkey Funeral Home chairs had been set up for the show. A clapboard stage spanned the distance between the two one-hundred-year oaks. The stage's jaunty awning jutted over the platform, and ramps, tied together in ropes, were looped artistically across the base.

In front, two red-necked men were getting redder-necked trying to get the sound equipment to work. Their mysterious jerky movements had attracted a band of slack-jawed children.

Gaily colored booths had been set up around the grounds and you could buy a wide assortment of vittles. Everything you bought, except the cakes and pies, came with a free handful of ramps.

Ramps are a distant cousin of the leek, which is a half-sister to the scallion or green onion. Take a bite of ramps and you know it. They are the Limburger cheese of the onion family. But they make mighty tasty fixin's in a green salad. The Cawkey County Ramp Festival now in its 63rd year, attracted folks from five counties. Sometimes a nationally known speaker would attend. One year the festival drew a U. S. President.

Mostly, though, it was just eating and drinking and country music. And ramps. And ramp fumes.

With your ramps, you could get fried chicken, hot hush puppies, corn on the cob. Sandwiches were great juicy chunks of baked ham, barbecued pork or roast beef—all on moist slabs of homebaked bread.

Uncle Muley got him a barbecued pork sandwich and a dope (the colloquial term for soda pop) and went over to sit down on one of the Purkey Funeral Home chairs. Some men were bringing the musical instruments up on the stage. There was a xylophone and a guitar and an accordion. Also there was the big bass drum which none of the Drums ever hit. It had "THE SINGING DRUMS" in red letters across the hitting part.

Uncle Muley finished his sandwich and promptly went to sleep with his mouth open. But before long, Gomer's Aunt Beulah had her sharp elbow in his lean ribs. "Come to, Mister. The show is about to start." All around Uncle Muley, the sea of funeral home chairs were now filled. Up front people were sitting two to a seat. Kids were perched in the next county. Then, Pastor Goins waddled onto the crates.

"I hope the Drums sing some of the oldies," grumbled Uncle Muley.

"Try to be modern and up to date," said Aunt Beulah.

"I like the oldies. Oldies like 'I Am Lying on My Piller, Looking at My Ceiling and Wondering What You Are Up To Tonight.' "

"That *is* a oldie," said Aunt Beulah.

Up on the stage, the loudspeaker gave a screech which was loud enough to jar the living daylights out of the souls in the next county. Then, Pastor Goins, waddled onto the stage, looking his usual chapped self. His shoes had sucked his socks into the rinds of his heels. The pastor put his mouth against the mike and shouted:

"IS THIS HERE THING WORKING YET?"

Uncle Muley grabbed at his ears.

"Don't take on so," Aunt Beulah said. "They will get going in a tad." The sound equipment gave off another whining hum before it settled down and Pastor Goins, now speaking in a reasonable voice, directed all assembled to bow down their heads in prayer. "Bless these ramps and bless this here ramp festival for which we are all gathered together for here today. May these ramps go to the strength of our bodies and may the strength of our bodies go to the Lord's work. . . ." He paused here, giving Uncle Muley false hopes that the prayer had ended. Shooting a sideways glance at Aunt Beulah and seeing her head still bowed, he sighed and studied his hands.

". . . But Lord teach us the meaning of Festival. Teach us to rejoice, but *teach us* to remember that we should not *overeat* or go in for gluttony . . ."

Uncle Muley leaned over to Aunt Beulah and whispered: "He always puts a damper on things."

"Shish, Mister."

The pastor droned on: "Help us, O Lord, to be temperate in all of our doings . . ."

"How," whispered Uncle Muley, "can a body be temperate about ramps?"

Aunt Beulah whispered back: "Can't you let the preacher get through one prayer without running off at the mouth?"

The preacher went on: "Help us, O Lord, to enjoy the fruits of this earth, but don't let us forget FROM WHOM

ALL BLESSINGS FLOW. And now, let us lift up our hearts in praise. With the strength in our limbs, with the blood in our veins and with the breath in our lungs . . ."

Uncle Muley nudged his wife. "If the Almighty was to get a whiff of our ramp breath, He might not want to have no truck with us."

"Shish Mister."

". . . And so Lord, teach us not to make pigs of ourselfs. Amen."

"Whoo," said Uncle Muley. "My neck was getting stiff."

Daddy Drum popped onto the stage like he had been shot from a catapult.

"I just love how he takes on," said Aunt Beulah, tilting her knockwurst toward Uncle Muley without taking her eyes off the stage.

"Hi there, you all," said Daddy Drum, waiting for the applause to melt away and patting the air with his outstretched hands to douse the clapping. Daddy Drum wasn't all that anxious for folks to stop clapping him, so while he was patting the air with his hands he was also clowning around, but the clapping eventually stopped. Daddy Drum sidled around to the left side of the mike and took his talky pose. "Well, folks, I don't know about you, but *I* been eatin' ramps!"

The crowd cheered.

"Yessir, ramps! Reckon I'll have to go down to the store and fetch me something to chew on to kill that smell . . . something like GARLIC!"

The crowd roared.

"All I know is," said Daddy Drum, "that my wife won't speak to me. Not that she's mad at me. She's just afraid that if she speaks to me, I'll speak back."

The crowd roared, hollered and wailed with glee.

"Not that ramps smell all that bad on your breath. 'Course, I did lean over a while ago to smell the rose in my wife's hair. And the dang rose wilted."

The crowd whooped with delight.

"On the other hand, I seen a bunny rabbit a little while ago. Hopping over the grass peaceful as anything. It didn't seem to notice nothing . . . 'Course it had on a GAS MASK!"

The crowd yukked and whistled and held its bellies.

"But I love ramps. I really do. 'Course I don't eat 'em often. I can prove I've not ate ramps OFTEN. I GOT EIGHT KIDS!"

People fell out of their seats. When the mirth died down after that, Daddy Drum asked: "Don't you know them?"

This extracted another numbing round of applause.

Then, one by one, each clapped in from the wings, were his eight offspring, appearing in order of seniority.

"Melody Belle!"

"Xylo Viola!"

"Clara Nettie."

"Mandy Lynn."

"Reveille Lullaby."

"Organ."

"Harmony Carol."

"And Hymn!" Hymn got a special roar of applause. He was his daddy's straight man.

"And now, boom, boom, for the prettiest Drum I ever met in my life . . . Mam Drum!"

The mother, looking not much older than the oldest strolled on stage, bowed and took her place. Daddy Drum squeezed her hand, dropped it and stepped up to the mike. He picked up a guitar and gave it a strum which meant that he was going to get serious, so the crowd sobered, wiped its eyes and caught its breath.

"Going to sing," said Daddy Drum "something all of us knows. For you folks out there who like to hear the oldies . . ."

Even Uncle Muley joined that clapping.

". . . we will sing the old favorite: 'There's A Big Surprise, By and By, Waiting for Me in the Evening Sky.' "

Uncle Muley was beside himself. It was his very favorite. He settled down. Roy Goodpasture turned up his hearing aid. Aunt Beulah jiggled her knockwurst curls as the sunlight played happily on the white rows of scalp that gleamed out between her curls.

The Singing Drums went to it. Away they whanged, their nasal voices irritating the delicate wiring in the sound equipment. Their high notes blew at the long strands of Christmas tree lights that had been strung up for decoration.

Their low notes were joined by a few dogs.

Aunt Beulah brushed away a tear. "They ought to be in pictures."

"Shish, Missus," said Uncle Muley.

When the Drums were finished there wasn't a dry eye in the crowd. They did one extra chorus, reducing everyone to blubber with their tinny strains and then Daddy Drum stepped out and said:

"Now to inject a little humor."

The folks dried their eyes and laughed.

"Yawl remember that old favorite: 'My Little Boy Has Outgrowed His First Sunday Pants'?" Oh, did they remember that oldie and while they whistled and stomped, Daddy Drum clowned some more. He turned around and playfully examined the cuffs of Hymn's good breeches.

The crowd howled at this. Hymn grinned back.

Then the Singing Drums jigged and jumped through "My Little Boy Has Outgrowed His First Sunday Pants."

M'am Drum, of course, took one of the choruses, solo, and this would have brought the house down if there had been a house to bring down. The folks clapped until their palms were bright pink.

Daddy Drum took over again. "Now, we've got a few surprises for you." (Pause) "Most of you good folks out there have been waiting on the postman these days to bring letters to you from Gomer Pyle and the boys."

"Land," said Aunt Beulah. "He named Gomer's name!"

On stage, Daddy Drum turned to Xylo Viola and she began to feed him the names of the other boys. Father and daughter engaged in a "comfy" little give-and-take—a homey bit of stage business that the crowd adored.

"Fat who?"

"Gorley."

"Oh. Well, anyway, the boys in Gomer's division."

"Platoon."

"Correction. Platoon. I can't get on to that military talk."

The folks loved that.

"Anyway, Xylo Viola has wrote her first song in honor of writing to the boys." He turned to beam at his second oldest. "Correction, she has wrote *two* songs. And I want her to sing them both right now. How about it Xylo Viola?"

Dreamy looking little Xylo Viola came forward floating on a tide of applause.

Uncle Muley whispered: "She looks good enough to eat with a spoon."

Keeping up the banter, Xylo Viola turned to her daddy. "Which one should I sing first."

"Save the best for last."

She nodded. "My first song, she said in a soft southern drawl, "is entitled 'The Mail Means a Little More Than a Little Letter to Me Anymore.' "

"See," said Aunt Beulah, "I told you she had gone sweet on that Sergeant Carter."

"Don't leap at conclusions, Missus."

Xylo Viola had a sweet little throaty voice, and it came out of her throat instead of her cute little nostrils. She was the only one of the Drums who didn't sound tinny. She also had a tantalizing way of moving her head and shoulders when she sang.

Her maiden composition was as follows:

(Verse one)
Anymore,
When the mailman comes knockin' at my door,
My pore heart is not achin' sore.
For anymore
They is letters galore
From one who has got the score.
(Verse two)
Anymore,
When the mailman comes ringin' at my bell,
I feel just awfully doggone swell
For anymore

I am here to tell
He loves me to a fare-thee-well.

Aunt Beulah nudged Uncle Muley. "See, listen to that. I tell you she has got her hat set for that Sergeant Carter."

"Songs is just made-up fiction. You can say anything in songs," whispered her mate.

Xylo Viola swung into the chorus:

The mail means more than a little letter to me anymore
'Cause I'm getting letters from a guy who has swore
To defend this country from that turrible cold war.
Oh, the mail means more than a little letter to me anymore.

Xylo Viola did another chorus, smiled sweetly for the clapping and went on to introduce her next song.

"I would like to dedicate this number to a *certain* sergeant, who is drill instructor of a *certain* platoon in a *certain* branch of the armed services." She smiled. "The song is called: 'I Have My Eye On Someone I've Never Seen.' "

Aunt Beulah poked Uncle Muley so hard he saw stars. "Now if that ain't plain as the nose on your face! She's stuck on that Sergeant Carter."

Thunder rumbled in the distance, and Uncle Muley poked his nose in the direction of heaven. "I smell rain," he said.

"Lord-a-mercy," said Aunt Beulah, her hands flying protectively to her curls. "My hair will come down."

"Come on, let's git," said Uncle Muley.

"Wait until the song is sung, Mister. I want to hear this one."

A few preliminary raindrops, big as nickels, landed on Uncle Muley's Sunday pants. He put a firm hand on Aunt Beulah and pulled her out of her seat. Aunt Beulah, torn between wanting to hear the song, and fear of having her hair come down, trotted obligingly after her spouse. She cocked her head now and again but she couldn't make out the words, although the tune was catchy.

When they got to the car, parked before the no-parking

sign, Uncle Muley tore up the traffic summons and dropped it into the rain-speckled dust. "I got no need of that."

On the way home, Gomer's Aunt Beulah crowed:

"Well, I was right about two things today. It did rain, and Xylo Viola has took a shine to that sergeant."

"Well, Missus, I allow about how you were right about the rain," said Gomer's Uncle Muley.

Chapter Eight

IN THE 72 HOURS before the arrival of Brig. Gen. Kenneth A. Cusps, the overfed platoon in Sgt. Harold Q. Carter's charge lost 52 of the collective 78 pounds it had gained.

Sgt. Carter brushed the stardust out of his eyes, limbered up his vocal cords, and became his normal on-duty self, which was testy as a boil. Orders came out of him like M-60 machine-gun bullets. He leapt and danced after his charges. And the hot July sun did not make any of it easier. It beat down like hammers.

"I can jest feel that sun meltin' at this here spare tire of flesh I'm carrying around my waist," said Gomer as they jogged through the countryside.

In the field, Ray had a field day complaining.

"We are all going to get enlarged hearts," he said.

At the onset of the 72-hour preparation for the Inspector General's visit, Ray had developed a full blown case of the I-Told-You-So's. "Told you this wouldn't last. Told you this was too good to be true. Told you we were going to have to pay for all that good food and pay with a pound of flesh."

"Seems to me," replied Gomer, who was not familiar with Shakespeare, "that we could pay for it with a mite more than a pound. We are downright chubby."

Ray moaned on about the danger of hernia and recited the case histories he remembered about sunstroke.

Gomer just grinned. It was Ray's like to complain. He complained because of exercise; he complained at the lack of exercise. He complained about work; he complained about the lack of work.

One day when he was off duty, Ray complained:

"The trouble with doing nothing is that you never know when you are finished."

Jim Holmes, on the other hand, liked all the noise inherent in any large scale scramble. So he jumped lithely through the paces Sgt. Carter had mapped out.

And Sgt. Carter had mapped out some lively paces. He drilled his men, then drilled them some more. He trotted them. He spelled them and then he ran them. He lectured them and then he worked them.

Sweat stood like pearls on their brows. Their green utilities were washed gray by perspiration.

Carter himself was sweating bazooka shells. He had always made a good showing in the annual inspection. He didn't want to bomb out this time. So he drilled his platoon some more.

Then marched it some more.

Then lectured it.

"These push-ups," said Gomer Pyle, "is giving me arm muscles as big as my Aunt Beulah's boiled potatoes."

The sergeant doubled the calisthenics. "Hut, du, three, four. Alllll-together, hut, du, three, four. Onnnnce again. Hut, du, three, four."

At bayonet practice, the sergeant wasn't happy until the heavy pugil sticks were swirling like batons. *"Plunge. Again. Go. Faster. Growl, Marine! Growl."*

Between drills, the men cleaned like they had never cleaned before. "I swanney," said Gomer. "I think I am getting dishpan hands."

The men polished everything down to and including the lids on the polish cans.

Said Gomer: "I never seen such a fuss since the time my

Uncle Muley got a mean streak and took it out on the local police."

While he cleaned his rifle, Gomer recalled how Uncle Muley, angry because the police had taken his driver's license away from him for the fourth time in two years, went down to the station in the dark of night and propped concrete blocks in back of all the squad car wheels.

"Then he shot out two windows at headquarters with his .45 and skeedaddled."

Jim Holmes stroked the flat back of his head. "Why'd they take his driver's license away from him?"

"Oh, they do that regular as clockwork. See, my Uncle Muley always parks by fireplugs."

"He does?"

"Sure," said Gomer. "They's always an open spot by a fireplug. You can't get it out of Uncle Muley's head that them spots ain't meant for him to park in."

Jim poked a reamer through the barrel of his rifle. "What happened after he shot out the police windows?"

"Well, they couldn't take out after him immediate because of them concrete blocks in back of their patrol car wheels, but, sure as shootin', they knowed who done it. They come after Uncle Muley at home. Pulled him out of bed." Gomer wagged his head to recall. "My Aunt Beulah had to come down to the jailhouse in her hair curlers to bail him out."

But the fuss caused by Uncle Muley paled by comparison to the fuss in Gomer's platoon. In scarcely 48 of the 72 hours, Sgt. Carter had got the old be-zap back into the close order drill. He had ironed the kinks out of M-14 rifle practice, and he had siphoned the molasses out of the performance of the obstacle course.

And in those 48 hours, Sgt. Carter had not lifted his pen once to write to Xylo Viola Drum. He tucked her away at the base of his brain next to his pituitary gland and turned the attention of his frontal lobes on the barracks.

'All right men," he said as he began to divide the chores. "You Gorley, hit the floors . . . Holmes take the windows. . . ." Ray got mattress detail. On it went, until Sgt.

Carter got to Gomer. "You, Pyle," he said, "see that all this stuff . . ." he swept an arm at the lockers full of toiletries and crates of oranges and grapefruit and canned meats, ". . . see that all of this stuff gets cleaned out of here."

Gomer's face fell. It was not that Gomer minded the work because he didn't. "Whut in the world am I going to do with all this stuff, Sergeant Carter?"

"THAT is your problem."

"Well, what do you reckon I should do, sir?"

Sgt. Carter could not order the men to destroy, sell, dump, or donate their personal property. But he could order them to remove it from the barracks. A Marine could have personal property, but where in the Marine Manual did it say he could have enough boodle to start a drugstore or open a delicatessen counter.

"I don't reckon ANYTHING," shouted the sergeant. He did not want Gomer to think he was ordering him to throw away the cans, tins, boxes, jars, crates and cartons of assorted goodies. But he hoped Gomer might reach that conclusion by himself. "Just get it out of the lockers, Pyle. OUT. Do you read me?"

"I read you loud and clear, Sergeant Carter, sir."

Gomer could not see throwing out good shaving cream when children were starving in India, so, as he hauled box after box out of the barracks, his mind sifted through an assortment of ideas.

"Waste is a sin," thought Gomer Pyle, who didn't want to be a sinner.

It was as he was walking past the supply hut that his mind snagged on *the* idea. There in front was the supply truck, newly unloaded, waiting for the dozens of empty ammo tins which it would haul back across several states to the main supply depot.

There, at the main depot, the boxes would be refilled and shipped out again to this or any other Marine base.

Why not, reasoned Gomer, send back a few vittles to the hard working men in the supply depot. The ammo boxes were going back empty. Why not send them back full?

Gomer walked around to the side of the hut and, sure

enough, there in all their empty splendor stood several dozen tins. Just about enough, thought Gomer. He fell to loading the ammo boxes with grapefruit, oranges, salami, toothpaste. . . .

Had the entire base not been in such a frenzy, someone might have seen him industriously putting grapefruit in grenade boxes.

In fact, when it came time for him to begin loading his "empties" on the supply truck, he *was* seen by a number of men, three of them officers. But all of them took the same notice of a recruit dutifully loading empties on a supply truck that they would have taken of a recruit dutifully peeling potatoes. It was the most normal thing in the world to see a recruit loading empties onto a supply truck.

His toil finished, Gomer went back to his barracks happy in his mind that on the other end of the line some unsuspecting fellows in the supply depot would fall heir to a treasure trove of food the likes of which they had never seen.

What Gomer did not know was that the ordnance officer, making one last check, climbed into the truck, and attempting to kick aside one of Gomer's "empty" boxes, realized that it was full. He climbed off the truck, sought out his sergeant, and raised hell with him.

"I thought I told you to get that truck unloaded!"

The sergeant sputtered. "I ordered it unloaded. Those are just empties."

"Empties eh? Go pick up that box and tell me if it's empty."

The sergeant obeyed. "Full," he admitted, scratching his head.

The stenciled lettering on the end of the box announced that it contained grenades. It felt like it contained grenades. He didn't question it.

"All right," snapped the ordnance officer. "Get busy and get those boxes off that truck and into the hut. And on the double."

Chapter Nine

BRIG. GEN. KENNETH A. CUSPS was tall with a ramrod stance and a neck like a giraffe with a golf ball lodged in it for an adam's apple. He had a kind face, cracked like old leather and permanently tanned from tens of combat missions in the broiling South Pacific.

He got out of the jeep, which for some strange reason he had driven himself—his chauffeur sitting proudly alongside in the passenger seat. Gen. Cusps looked around at the manicured grass in front of the administration building and nodded with pleasure. The inspection tour was off to a good start.

He gazed at the blue steel-roofed barracks—each brick in their facades newly scrubbed. He glanced down at the polished concrete walks, looked up at the sparkling jeeps and shining trucks and nodded with satisfaction to note that all the trees seemed properly pruned.

Not a blade of grass crawled over the curbs. The hedges in the central mall had been clipped with care and stood at attention. The American flag fluttered straight out, catching the breeze of this late July day and rippling gently at full spread.

The camp was, the general thought pleasantly, in apple pie order.

A tour of the base bore out his initial impression.

The desks in the office units were spotless; the bunks in the barracks were so taut you could bounce a dime off them; the tables in the mess hall were so clean you could have eaten off them.

Officers' quarters were immaculate. The push ball field had been rolled. The rifle targets had been newly painted. The camp chapel glistened in the cleanliness which was next to Godliness.

The eagle on the Marine emblem over the door of the

main building looked as though it had never seen a pigeon. Wings stretched, it perched atop the polished globe and anchor. The words 'Semper Fidelis" streamed from its mouth on a band so spanking clean it hurt the general's eyes.

Then, before his ramrod person, came unit after unit of smartly stepping men, the creases in their dress-blues sharp enough to cut sausage.

The general reviewed the troops, his pleasure mounting.

At the rifle range, he watched closely as the men, synchronized tighter than the works of a Swiss watch, loaded, aimed, fired . . . loaded, aimed, fired.

Regis-Ray was the top marksman on the base.

Gomer said it was because he had a handicap to overcome like "that feller who put pebbles in his mouth to get over the stutters."

Ray's handicap was his wide-apart eyes. He was so accustomed to the wide-angle view he had of life that when he closed one eye to aim, he lost his bearings. So he had to aim with both eyes, and adjust the service rifle a degree or so to the left to take up the slack between his far-flung orbs. The result got him every marksman's medal the outfit gave.

Sgt. Carter had Ray perform solo for the general and the general was so pleased he could hardly contain himself.

Then, over lunch at the officers' mess, the general spoke of his desire to see some action on the combat range. It was an unorthodox request, but Gen. Cusps didn't win beachheads by orthodox methods.

He said he wanted to see a few platoons in action at Combat Range 303. It was a new range; had gone into operation only two months earlier and was designed to give troops a variety of simulated battle experience. Gen. Cusps said he wanted to see how the range operated.

Of course, that wasn't the whole reason. The general was downright sick and tired of being assigned to inspection teams. He wanted the smell of battle again.

At Combat Range 303, he planned to stand in the tower and direct the "enemy" action against the charging Marines.

The tower was equipped with a panel which controlled forty pop-up enemy soldiers, thirteen machine-gun simulators, two artillery simulators, and ninety demolition charges on a combat range covering three miles square and divided into three separate sections—each with different terrain and obstacles.

It was an ingenious operation. Press a button and out on one of the fields a thin wooden human figure popped up. They were electrically controlled to fall and rise with each hit by rifle fire. Enemy casualty down and replacement up in one impulse. A recording device in each pop-up figure relayed each hit to the control tower where it was tallied.

The machine guns operated on bottled propane gas and oxygen. A spark plug ignited the volatile gas and out came a "rattattattaa" that could curl the hair of any fighting man. Demolition to simulate incoming artillery and mortar fire was set up in nine fields just off the course.

Gen. Cusps' request was irregular, but the Marines were Semper Fidelis and Semper ready. Orders were snapped, the troops changed into battle gear, ammo boxes were hauled out of the supply hut and three platoons of men and supplies were loaded into trucks and driven to Combat Range 303.

Sgt. Carter felt both mixed pride and apprehension that his platoon was one of the three chosen for this extemporaneous afternoon exercise.

He knew that Ray's marksmanship had something to do with it. It was one thing to hit a target at 500 yards with a tight sling and a good position. It was another to score highly on the combat range qualification course. Jim Holmes was undoubtedly another reason for the choice. Big, strapping Jim loved pelting things with grenades. Fearless, he would romp into a nest of simulated machine guns and blow simulated terror out of it.

Carter's apprehension centered around Pyle. Granted Pyle didn't jiggle his rifle every which way any more. Granted Pyle had improved. Still, Carter would have been happier if Gomer had put in for sick bay.

The general strode out of the officers' mess, again relegated his waiting chauffeur to the passenger seat and set out for the range. Jogging and bouncing through the sunlit countryside, the old battle-hungry leatherneck loved every bump and grind the jeep delivered.

He filled his old combat-starved lungs with gulps of dust and fairly ached to get to the site and watch the men fall on an imaginary enemy. He began to whistle the Marine Hymn in anticipation.

Of the three divisions at the combat range, one was to train the Marines to advance under heavy fire; another was to give them practice in hilly terrain; the third—the toughest—was underbrush combined with open field, and included sniper fire from a practice hut.

Red Owl Platoon had been assigned to Course A, where it would advance under heavy artillery mortar and machine gun fire. Blue Fox would try Course B with the hilly terrain, and Green Serpent, Sgt. Carter's platoon, would slither through the underbrush, break into the clearing in a "quick fire attack" and capture the practice hut.

All three courses involved advancing under some fire and execution of open field marksmanship. In all three, the pop-up targets would leap at the men at the whim of the range coordinator in the tower. But it was Carter's platoon which would rush the practice hut, plagued by pop-ups and hindered by underbrush. His men would have to advance with both rifles and hand grenades and with little or no covering fire.

Platoons Red Owl and Blue Fox received 100 rounds of M-14 rifle ammo per man, plus rifle grenades and ammo for the M-79s to be used when the troops needed something heavier than rifle fire. The small-arms ammo was live; the M-79 rounds contained only a propellant charge. When its turn came up, Green Serpent Platoon was to get 150 rounds of M-14 rifle ammo per man, plus the inert hand grenades.

Platoon Red Owl assembled at the departure line while enemy artillery shells were set to burst overhead. The artillery simulators were briefed by an umpire in the same manner as a platoon leader is briefed when his unit is part of a large attacking force.

The men in the other two platoons were standing around the edge of the range, watching the exercises to benefit from the performance of the others.

Jim Holmes let out a joyous shout when the first artillery shell boomed, exploding a curtain of smoke which made a fitting backdrop for the opening exercise of the afternoon. Gomer Pyle's mouth jogged open, and Carter barked above the machine gun fire, "Look sharp men."

Up in the tower Gen. Cusps was standing in front of the panel giving orders to the range-coordinator who pressed the buttons and flipped the switches that set off the "enemy" defense.

"Two on the left," commanded Gen. Cusps, bringing two more explosions of artillery on the left flank of the attacking platoon.

"Pop-up on point three," he roared, triggering four pop-up enemies into sight.

"Down on three," commanded the general, indicating that the charging Marines had hit two pop-up enemies as indicated by the red lights on the panel. The general glowed with excitement. The Marines were attacking like seasoned combat veterans. The range was now shrouded in swirling smoke. In the tower, the range-coordinator, on command from Gen. Cusps, was pushing buttons which set up the wooden pop-ups, discharged demolition shells and triggered the machine-gun emplacements whose sound effects seemed to send live, deadly bullets streaming across the field.

Under the fire, the men snaked and scrambled. Out into the tall grass they crawled, almost walking on their elbows. Their battle dress was soaked with sweat and smeared with dirt. Rifles cracked. Bayonets flashed in the sun. Gen. Cusps could hardly contain himself. He directed artillery, machine gun and mortar fire on the advancing green wave, but nothing stopped it. It was Tarawa all over again.

Cheers rose from the spectator platoons who were standing out of range and watching the swirling action. As soon as Red Owl marched away from the firing area, targets were collected and hits recorded. Ammo was turned in and counted. The marksmanship efficiency factor in scoring was determined by comparing the number of hits with the number of rounds used.

Then Blue Fox was issued its ammo and troops moved over to Course B. There Blue Fox scrambled up the hill and shot away at the pop-ups. Again the cheers from the spectator platoons. The range exercises were proceeding flawlessly.

Gen. Cusps, in a froth of excitement, relinquished his command in the tower. He wanted to see Green Serpent perform from the ground. Hopping into his jeep he whipped over to Course C where Sgt. Carter's platoon was to resume the action.

Gen. Cusps was particularly anxious to see how Marksman Ray would perform under these conditions. Generals had hassled over this question for generations. On one side were men who said there was no point in teaching combat marksmanship on a formal, known-distance shooting range. It was an artificial situation, they said. On the other side were the men who said you have to sharpen the eye and train the muscles first before they are turned loose for combat marksmanship. Since Ray was an exceptional marksman on a formal, known-distance range, the general was anxious to see how he would perform in combat, struggling through underbrush, nagged by sniper fire and surprised by pop-ups.

Gen. Cusps was discussing the question with a colonel and two captains near the departure line of Course C while Sgt. Carter's men were issued their ammo.

Then something went wrong.

It was hard to tell what it was at first. The men, so highly organized a moment before, now broke into little nervous, disconsolate groups.

Ray, whose natural nose for trouble smelled it instantly, felt a certain lift at the prospect of it. Jim Holmes, who couldn't wait to blast the practice hut with the grenades, resented any delay, no matter what was causing it.

What was causing it was soon apparent. It was the supplies.

The general, piqued at this flaw in an otherwise perfect day, and annoyed to have the anticipated maneuver left dangling in front of him like a carrot, marched briskly over to the center of the confusion.

The center of confusion, at that moment, was a box of grenades. The general stepped staunchly over to the box, dipped in his steady old hand and pulled out a pink grapefruit.

For a very long moment, the general just stood staring down at the pink grapefruit. It was a fine grapefruit, large, firm and round with a smooth blushing skin. Gen. Cusps knew it was a pink grapefruit because it said "Pink" on the skin.

Cautiously, he dipped his hand into the grenade box once again and up came a sister to the first fruit. The grapefruit growers of Florida had developed this special strain of fruit so that it would look nice, sliced in half, the edges scalloped, the top sugared and soaked in Cointreau, then placed under an open flame to sear those edges and served as a grand dessert.

The general upended the grenade box and out tumbled a dozen grapefruit. They rolled gaily on the dirt, adding a bright, pinkish-yellow touch to the sun-caked earth. The general watched, fascinated as the yellow orbs rolled and dipped and came to a halt. He opened another grenade box and out rolled two dozen navel oranges. A third box stowed another round of grapefruit, which he upended and sent wobbling over the embattled ground.

The tanned general—his complexion now highly tinged with red, stood emplanted in a fruit bowl of Vitamin-C-enriched pink grapefruit and jumbo size navel oranges.

Sputtering with rage, he spun on the disorganized men and roared:

"WHO IS RESPONSIBLE FOR THIS?"

A major moved quickly forward to say something, stepped on a grapefruit, pirouetted in the air, and fell to the ground, spraining his ankle. He was the first casualty of the war games.

A captain rushed to help the fallen man, stepped on two jumbo oranges which served nicely as ball bearings, propelling him forward with exceptional speed. He landed with a thud on three pink grapefruit, squishing the juices out of their bursting skins, and squirting grapefruit juice into the eyes of three lieutenants, blinding them.

The general viewed the battlefield with dismay. One major, one captain and three lieutenants lay felled in the Battle of the Citrus Fruits. About them, immobilized, stood a company of battle-trained Marines, afraid to move forward into the juicy mine field.

He stood ramrod straight, the golf ball in his giraffe-like throat bouncing up and down. Over the field of carnage hung the delicious aroma of freshly-squeezed orange juice. And all was silent. You could hear the butterfly wings as they fluttered over pollen-laden clover. Off in the distance, a black crow wheeled against the Wedgewood-blue sky, cawed, and swooped over a field of golden ripening corn. Queen Anne's lace and wild daisies bent their heads to a gentle breeze. A lonesome cow, far away, mooed.

Shattering the quiet, the general bawled:

"CAN ANYONE EXPLAIN THIS?"

A small voice in the rear piped:

"No sir, I cain't."

Heads pivoted in unison. Gomer Pyle stood as rigid as his rifle, eyes looking out straight ahead from under his camouflage helmet.

Sgt. Carter started to lunge for Gomer. This was no time for casual conversation. But Carter froze when he saw Gomer's mouth already working. "See, General, I'm the guilty party, but I sure can't explain it. It's as big a mystery to me as it is to you."

Indeed it was. Gomer had no idea how those grenade boxes full of fruit had got back into the supply shed. He had loaded the "empties" on the truck himself.

The general snapped: "Where is your D.I.?"

"Oh, it's not his fault," piped Gomer.

"H-here, here I am, sir," said Sgt. Carter stepping gingerly forward and standing between two mangled oranges.

"Do you have any idea what your man is talking about?"

"No sir."

"How did this fruit get into those grenade boxes?"

"I have no idea sir."

"Where did you GET the ammo boxes?"

"From ordnance, sir, like all the others."

"Did you see anyone tamper with them?"

"No, sir. I did *not, sir.*"

The general had heard enough. He told Sgt. Carter and the colonel to report to him in the conference room at 1600 hours.

Then, the general, stepping cautiously through the spilled fruit, left the battlefield.

Chapter Ten

WHY

The general wanted to know why.

The colonel said he didn't know why. He asked Sgt. Carter: "Why?"

Sgt. Carter, who felt like he had just swallowed a swarm of bees, said he didn't know why.

"Then who DOES know why?" the general wanted to know.

The colonel looked at Sgt. Carter. Sgt. Carter looked back at the colonel. They both looked at the general.

The general, who had calmed down somewhat, sighed. "You checked with ordnance?"

The colonel nodded: "Several more boxes have . . . uh . . . various non-ammo materials in them."

"Such as?"

"Shaving cream. Pickled pigs' feet." The colonel cleared his throat nervously. "We're launching an investigation right away. Generally—even with the competitive spirit among the men—pranks don't take this sort of turn. . . ."

The general waved him silent. "Who was the recruit who stood forward out in the field and took the blame for this?"

Both the colonel and the sergeant answered in perfect unison:

"Gomer Pyle."

Then the colonel said: "But Carter's platoon has no entree to the supply hut."

"No one checked with this recruit . . . this Pyle?"

The colonel nodded. "We plan to."

"Send for him now," said the general. "At least he was man enough to speak out. Besides, I'd like to hear how he explains this."

The colonel said that he, too, would like to hear how Gomer explained the mysterious ammo boxes. Sgt. Carter said, yes, he'd like to hear Gomer's explanation.

Gomer's explanation, of course, was not an easy flowing narrative. It opened with a discourse in praise of Sgt. Carter and a plea to absolve the sergeant of all blame. It waxed eloquent on what Sgt. Carter had taught him in the brief time he had been in the Marines. It was laced through with Gomer's sympathy for the sergeant, whose job it was to deal with Gomer, and who, according to Gomer, was trying his level best to teach Gomer to be a good Marine. For all of this Gomer was, he said, most appreciative.

The general, who was at the core a kind and patient man, listened as Gomer pursued a second round of testimonials for the squirming sergeant. Then Gomer paused.

"But I reckon you want to know how them vittles got into them supply boxes."

The general nodded yes, because, yes, that was precisely what he wanted to know.

"Well, sir. I put them there. Now I reckon you want to know why I put them there. Well, sir, I put them there so as not to throw them into the garbage because waste is a sin and children is starving in India."

Silence surrounded Gomer.

"Go on," said the general.

"Yessir. Well, see, sir. I figured as how, rather than send them supply tins back empty, I might as well put all that good food and good toilet supplies into them because somebody back in the supply depot could make good use of them things. And I swear to goodness, General Cusps, sir, I don't for the life of me know how them 'empties' got back off that truck and into the ordnance hut."

That someone had mistaken them for a new shipment was obvious, but the general didn't bother to enlighten Gomer. "Just tell me how you got all that food in the first place. All that shaving cream. Why? How?"

Gomer grinned. "Well, it all started because the fellers was feelin low about not gettin' no mail . . ."

Sgt. Carter squirmed and blew a fly off the tip of his nose. He hoped Gomer wouldn't tell the whole story.

But Gomer went back to the very beginning and told the whole story, editing scarcely a detail. He told the general about the morale being down because the recruits thought no one cared about them in peacetime. He wound back over the letter he sent to the church and the way the folks in Sinking Springs responded. He told about the beginnings of the food onslaught and how the recruits' mothers had got into the act. And he didn't omit any of the relatives of the recruits and how they had unleashed a new flood of goodies. He included the bake sale and the sociable and he ended:

"So, see folks does care about servicemen in time of peace."

The general blinked. He had never in all of his years of combat—in all of his years in the Pentagon—in all of his years in the service of his country in war and in peace—he had never heard anything quite like Gomer Pyle's story.

His old warrior's heart pumped with the patriotism of his fellow Americans. Why, it was simply the most heart-warming thing he had ever encountered.

Gone was the last vestige of his anger. Almost forgotten was his keen disappointment at not being able to see the Green Serpent Platoon in action.

The general felt strangely purged.

The fact remained, however, that Gomer, good intentions or not, was at fault for putting non-military supplies in military crates. The general said he would let Sgt. Carter mete out whatever punishment he felt was necessary. Turning back to Gomer, the general said:

"Now, Pyle, tell me about Sinking Springs."

Asking Gomer to talk about Sinking Springs was like turning a hose on yourself, and both Sgt. Carter and the colonel steeled themselves.

But Gomer was suddenly the soul of decorum. "Prettiest little place you ever saw," said Gomer. "Full of the best cooks a body . . ." he broke off. "You ever taste sweet 'tater pie, General?"

The general said he had not, but that he would like to.

"I'd be proud to go get you a wedge," said Gomer. "We just got some in the mail this morning."

To the everlasting surprise of everyone, however, the general got out of his chair. "I'll come with you," he said. "We'll ride in my jeep. It's just outside."

In his jeep, waiting faithfully outside was Larry R. Moran, Sergeant, USMC, a man uniquely *un*qualified to be the general's chauffeur. Sgt. Moran could not drive. He had never learned to drive; had never had a desire to learn to drive; and had never, through some miracle, been pressed by any necessity, large or small, to drive.

Had not his own boot camp and subsequent Marine training made a hard, strong and better man of him (as it is pledged to do), Larry R. Moran might not have withstood the initial shock when he was assigned to be the general's chauffeur.

Naturally, he had not put in for any such duty. He had requested office work, specifically public information. Somewhere in the not too distant past, in a test or on a form or in an oral admission, Sgt. Moran had honestly owned up to his inability to drive. Somewhere he had told someone that he could not drive, steer, manipulate or otherwise control any automobile, car, jeep, truck (stick or automatic) or any sort of gasoline- or diesel-powered means of motor transportation.

On his aptitude questionnaire he had claimed a shining proficiency in public relations. He did have some small experience in that line, for having gone through two years of college and having prepared himself for nothing, Larry had no choice but to secure work on a newspaper in the few months before the draft closed in.

Then just after he had decided to beat the draft and join the Marines, he fell in love with a Class 2 clerk-typist in the Department of the Interior in Washington, D.C. His goal became, immediately, to get close to the girl. His only chance was in Marine public information.

His bleat to be located in the Washington office of public information fell on deaf ears, not a phenomenon in any branch of the service.

Larry brandished his skimpy newspaper experience like a flaming sword, but it got him nowhere.

Typical of the services, he got the last thing he expected: chauffeur duty. But what he did not realize at the outset was that he had been chosen, hand-picked by the general specifically because he could NOT drive.

The general, for all of his bravery in combat, and for all of his well-rounded, intelligent bearing, had one weakness: he could not stand to be driven. If he was in a motor vehicle, he could not feel at ease unless he was behind its wheel. With someone else driving, Gen. Cusps reflectively tried to hit the brakes by slamming his foot against the floor board. By no means did he want anyone to discover his weakness, so rather than have anyone suspect, he accepted the succession of good drivers assigned him. He managed to see that they, shortly, got choice duty elsewhere. One he had busted. That was a former race driver.

Then he had found Larry R. Moran.

Larry had no aversion to being driven. He had no aversion to being driven by the general or by anyone else. He would far rather have been in Washington pecking out handouts and making plans to see his girl, but as work went this was certainly soft enough.

All that was required of him was that he wait in the driver's seat until the general appeared at the jeep or at any car he might be driving. The general would say: "Sergeant, I think I'll drive this time."

Larry would say: "Yes sir!" hop out of the driver's seat and into the passenger seat and off they would go.

Larry was good company; he was easy to talk to. He shot fear into the general's heart, however, when he pined out loud for duty in public information. Larry would wistfully moan how he missed news . . . how he longed to sit at the typewriter again even if it was only to grind out handouts. He had never ground out a handout in his life but he felt sure he could match the low caliber of the handouts issued from any government operation. He could, he felt sure, fade into the woodwork.

More important, he wanted to fade into the arms of the Class 2 clerk-typist. Her memory robbed him of any satisfaction he garnered in having a job which required nothing of him. For, next to his urge to rest was his urge to work as little as possible. A spot in public information would satisfy both urges.

The general soothed his own conscience with the realization that Larry didn't really have the stuff of a writer. He could scarcely write a coherent shopping list, much less a memo.

So he kept Larry on as chauffeur and tried to humor him now and again. And the general kept his mind open. If Larry ever showed any inkling of a talent for putting a verb in its proper place in a sentence, he might reconsider.

Larry's mind was on the Class 2 clerk-typist when the door swung open and the general, the colonel, the sergeant and Gomer Pyle came out. All were smiling.

Dutifully, Larry got out of the driver's seat and stood by the jeep.

"Sergeant," said the general, walking up to him briskly, "did you ever taste sweet potato pie?"

Larry was ready to say "Yes sir, I don't mind if you drive," when he realized that wasn't the question.

"Uh . . . uh . . ."

"Well, you are going to taste it now," he said turning to

Sgt. Carter and the others, "Climb in," he said. "I think I'll drive."

Sgt. Carter spoke up. "Why don't I drive sir. I'm familiar with where the barracks are and . . ."

"Good idea!" boomed the general and Larry Moran blinked. Had his chief lost his marbles?

"The colonel and I and Pyle here will walk, eh men? The walk will do us good, won't it Colonel?"

"Right, sir," said the colonel who would much rather have been in the jeep.

As Sgt. Carter turned the jeep's ignition key, Larry Moran noticed that his hand shook. "Rough session in there?" he asked his peer.

Carter ground the jeep into reverse and shot it out of its parking place. "A close shave, but the general . . . man, what a swell guy. He dropped the whole thing when he found out . . ."

Into the ears of Larry R. Moran, Sgt. Carter poured the whole story of the Sinking Springs packages, the patriotism and the recruit who had started the whole thing. Little did Carter know that the story was going into ears primed to snatch at anything that might make their owner look like public relations material. And this wasn't just anything. Ill-equipped as he was to recognize a story, Larry recognized this obvious one.

The Gomer Pyle story was a good enough public relations gimmick to win him a transfer, that is, if he could make the general aware of that.

He lost no time in making a stab at convincing the general. As soon as the general was back at the wheel, some candied yam lingering on his left cheek, Larry began his pitch.

"General, sir, I was thinking about that . . . uh . . . thing out there on the combat range today."

"I'd much rather NOT think of it, if you don't mind."

"How the whole thing ended, I mean," said Larry. "You know. It makes you think there's something to the old saying that you can lose a battle and win a war."

"How's that?"

"Sir, I was thinking that you might have lost that simulated battle today and really won a big victory for the Corps."

"You've lost me in the thicket, Sergeant."

"It's like this, sir. We always have to think of the morale of our men. The Corps knows how important it is to keep the men reasonably happy. And to keep their families happy. It's a 24-hour-a-day, year-round job for those lucky guys up there in public relations to keep the public posted on the Corps so we can get recruits and keep putting our best feet forward." Larry could not talk much better than he could write, but he was making a valiant effort. "They have to keep making the Corps look good—look its best."

"So you suggest we tell them about the battle of the grapefruit?"

"Oh, no sir, General. But I think the Corps would be missing a real bet if it didn't let the country know about Gomer Pyle and Sinking Springs. How patriotic that community is. How grateful the Corps is for that patriotism. It will call a lot of attention to the Corps."

"That it might," said the general hesitantly.

Striking while the iron was warm, Larry went on:

"Think of how proud all the Marine mothers will be when they hear that their sons are so admired that even strangers send them pies and cookies and salamis. The dads will be happy too, but the mothers, they're always worried that their sons will be turned into ruthless, blood-thirsty monsters, all gung-ho and no soul. The Sinking Springs folks don't think so. To them, our Marines are brave, patriotic BOYS who miss their apple pie and pigs' feet."

The general was beginning to shake his head negatively. "I don't know, sergeant, it's . . ."

Larry R. Moran, thinking of his clerk-typist, plunged on:

"See, the people of Sinking Springs know how important Marines are even in peacetime. How vital they are to our defense."

"Ummmmm," said the general.

Larry had heard the word "image" used in public relations so he hurled that out in his next broadside. "And what about America's image abroad. Think how the Russians will look at this and the Hungarians, the Albanians, the Red Chinese. American fighting men are tough and ready but they're not warmongers. American people are not apathetic and lazy. They stand behind their men even in peace. Americans are just as patriotic in peacetime as in wartime.

"Marines have more on their mind than M-14 rifles. They're just boys who like apple pie. And people—the people of this country—have more on their mind than their crabgrass and their job security. Don't you see, General?"

The general did indeed see, but he was secretly mourning what he saw. He was going to lose Larry Moran.

Larry raced on:

"Look, General, we've been criticized. We Americans have been accused . . . at this very moment we are being ridiculed for our materialism. Our enemies—yes, even our allies—say all we want is the 360-horsepower car, the split-level house in the suburbs, a four-week vacation with pay, and then forget everybody and anybody. They talk about Americans standing around and doing nothing while an old man is knifed in the street. That's the image they have of Americans—selfish, cold, indifferent—people who won't get INVOLVED! Now, here's a chance for the Marines to show the world that we Americans are deeper than that . . . that we Americans *do* get involved . . . that we Americans *do* care about our fellow men."

The general didn't know Larry had it in him. Neither did Larry.

It was a sad and difficult decision for the general to make, but a Marine officer like Brig. Gen. Cusps is a product of Marine officer training which produces hard, resilient men, who are flexible and self-reliant, men who know how to swallow defeat and come up fighting.

Losing Larry as a chauffeur would be a great loss. But a Marine officer must be honest and fair. He must be stern in the face of adversity. Losing Larry was adversity, but Gen. Cusps was stern in the face of it.

That next morning, he put through transfer papers assigning Larry R. Moran to the Office of Public Information in Washington, D.C.

His first assignment: The Gomer Pyle Story.

Chapter Eleven

THE UNITED STATES OF AMERICA was in its late summer doldrums.

Hub-cap thefts were on the decline.

Television re-runs had made the equivalent of eighteen orbits around the earth. The terrible three-year-olds who memorize nursery rhymes and can "read" them back word-for-word if you produce the picture book, were starting to repeat the dialogue of the TV re-runs.

Air conditioners wheezed and sweated. Heat rash flourished.

The kids were home from camp and were too lazy to nag their mothers or even to ask: "What can I do now, Mom?" Ice cream sticks littered the streets. Fruit ade mixtures and flower-seed packets bloomed in slow moving grocery carts.

In offices, banks, and business houses, the languor and lassitude were so pronounced that no one was bothering secretaries any more.

In the nation's newspaper offices, more than the usual number of words were misspelled. Men in sweaty shirts took more than their accustomed liberties with the truth.

News photographers, like slugs, inched around the cities in droopy-eyed search of hot weather pictures. The sun was so bright that the film exposed itself while still inside their film holders.

Copy editors tossed to see who would be sent to the pencil sharpener. The wire copy was dull. Worse, the humidity had made it soggy. Instead of responding with a crisp rip, it came off its machine with a slurp. The copy boys had to knead it off the machines.

Reporters slumped before their typewriters pecking at monotonous weather stories. News fit to be printed was not worth the bother. Good stories were as hard to find as ulcer-free city editors.

If the newspapers were hungry for stories, the local radio and television stations, which normally fed on the leavings of the local papers, were ravenous.

Then, along with a lively electric storm in the east, a high pressure system moving into the north, a drenching rain in the Plains states, and a general drop in the humidity, the Gomer Pyle story hit the news desks.

Larry R. Moran's story was no great shakes. It was full of clichés and bad grammar. It was over-emphasized where it should have been under-emphasized and vice versa. But it was edited by a lieutenant who corrected the spelling and grammar. A captain straightened out some of the syntax. A major took what little life there was in it out of it. A colonel put the lead in the third paragraph and a general put it in the fourth paragraph.

Then the Corps sent out 1,056 copies of the handout along with 1,056 machine-print glossies, 8 x 10, of Sgt. Carter's platoon standing at attention. In the right hand, instead of the rifle, each recruit held in his stiffly angled, platter-like palm, a cake or a pie or a tin of meat. Up front stood Gomer Pyle and Gen. Cusps eating a huge slice of devil's food cake while barely managing big smiles.

Editors did not normally peruse a punk handout. Nor did they read farther than the first paragraph if the article seemed dull. But they were so starved for a story of any kind that they scooped up the lousy handout and dug through the chaff. They were anxious for anything, and this, they found, as they untangled the governmentese and unhooked the militarese, was one wow of a story.

They scratched their front-page layout sheets.

"Make over," they shouted as they hurled the 8 x 10 glossies at their picture editors, who were so famished for art of any kind that they scrambled to attention.

"Re-write!" barked the editors, thus bringing their banks of hibernating re-write men out of a long summer's slumber.

The switchboards came to life as calls were placed to Washington to get more details and to Gomer's base to get quotes and more color.

"Get a local angle!" was the order as reporters were dispatched to the homes of the recruits, anyone who knew any of the recruits, or anyone who knew anyone who knew any of the recruits.

Local Marine recruiting offices were invaded and their surprised sergeants milked for their reactions.

"Oh, I think it is just great," was the quote that went into more than one reporter's notebook.

Mothers of Marines were interviewed. Fathers of Marines were interviewed. Mothers of prospective Marines were interviewed. Fathers of prospective Marines were interviewed.

Then, mothers of prospective soldiers were interviewed to find out why their sons were going to the Army instead of the Marines. The sons themselves were blushingly photographed at the Army recruiting stations.

Anything for a local angle. Some papers were lucky enough to find some boys who had switched to the Marines on the basis of being interviewed by a reporter.

"Well, now that I hear of all this good treatment in the Marines, I'm switching over," said Sam Slacch of Newark, New Jersey.

In towns unfortunate enough to not have a Marine recruiting office, the papers used the fact that they did NOT have a Marine Recruiting office as their local angle.

Some papers did man-on-the-street interviews. "What do you think about this little town, Sinking Springs?"

"Oh, I think it's fine."

"Do you think people ought to write to the Marines."

"Uh, yeah."

It was news.

The metropolitans ran it big, either at the bottom of

page one or at the top of their break pages. One New York tabloid covered its entire front page with the handout picture. A Queens shopping news interviewed Jim Holmes' aunt at her funeral home and photographed her standing under her marquee which announced today's dead.

In all 1,052 papers used it. Holdouts were four Midwest isolationist papers, which were so isolationist they refused to print anything about any international outfit even if it was their own international defense force.

And if the 1,052 papers were delighted, radio and television were incoherent with joy. With the still picture as a backdrop, they interviewed anybody local who could say anything at all about the Marines.

A few enterprising stations buttonholed chefs and, sitting them before the still picture of the platoon and its cakes and pies, had them describe pickled pigs' feet, sweet potato pie and a few other delicacies.

One station interviewed a psychologist about morale . . . morale in general, and Marine morale in particular, and good morale versus bad morale.

"Would you say that a happy man is a better fighting man?"

"Wull, yes and no. Too happy, of course, and he can, of course, get euphoric, of course."

"The thing to do then is to strike a happy balance?"

"Balance, yass."

"Well, sir, then how do we go about striking this happy balance?"

"Wull, it is different according to the particular person's individual psyche. In some cases it would take more than in other cases. In some cases it would take less. I would hesitate to say without seeing the patient."

"Thank you very much."

In Washington, senators were interviewed about patriotism and they were for it.

In San Francisco, a group of teenage activists was questioned about military service.

In Chicago, the USO baked some sweet potato pie for the servicemen.

And then, mysteriously and strangely, madly and zanily, the "Mail to Camp" craze hit the nation. There was a run on wrapping paper, mailing cartons and twine as aroused Americans everywhere took up the craze.

It made no more sense than the yo-yo craze or the hula-hoop insanity, or tight Chino pants, or the twist, or the frug.

But suddenly, everybody was doing it.

Teenagers flipped. You were "in" if you mailed to Gomer Pyle. It was as old-fashioned as the jitterbug; old-fashioned as the pictures of Dad in World War II; old-fashioned as a Ruby Keeler movie, a Tiffany lamp, a Flash Gordon comic book.

Hand-stenciled sweatshirts appeared overnight bearing the inscription: "I Mailed."

It was camp! It was camp to mail a package to camp. It was like mailing to the old boys of World War II. It was so far out that it was in.

Stand-up comics played on it. Broadway plays quickly worked it into their lines.

The U.S. Post Office experienced Christmas in August. Letters and do-not-bend envelopes with pictures flooded Sgt. Carter's besieged men. Extra postal help was hired. Private trucks were added to the fleet of parcel post trucks as packages began to mingle with the letters and the big brown envelopes.

Mothers sent cookies.

Fathers sent company-engraved pens.

Little boys sent marbles and bits of string.

The motor-scooter crowd sent its old license plates and emblems from foreign cars. Cherished all.

Good cooks sent cakes. Bad cooks sent cakes.

But mostly it was letters.

Widows sent letters of proposal.

Children sent poems.

Old people sent greeting cards.

Travelers sent postcards.

Little girls sent crayoned pictures.

Second graders in Bible Class sent Bible verses.

And teenage girls sent pictures, pictures, pictures. And letters, letters, letters.

The entire nation, no question about it, had come out of its doldrums.

Chapter Twelve

ON THE FIRST morning of the national mail avalanche, Gomer alone got 10,693 letters and 1,223 packages, 903 marriage proposals, a can of peanut brittle and an insured, special delivery airmail from his friend, Menlo.

It was in Menlo's letter that Gomer got his first inkling that something serious might be developing between Sgt. Carter and Xylo Viola Drum.

Menlo wrote:

"I am sending this letter special delivery and insured not just because the news included herein (and do I have news?) is all that important—though *we* think it's important—but because I figured with everybody writing to you, ordinary mail must be pretty common. Well, anyway . . .

"Here is what has happened. Xylo Viola Drum has got kind of sweet on your sergeant. I thought you might be interested to know that. As you seem to think the world and all of Sergeant Carter, we are all happy as can be that they seem to be hitting it off in the mail.

"And hitting it off they are. Things has took a serious turn in their relationship. Listen to this. *Xylo Viola has sent Sergeant Carter her appendix* . . . the one she had operated a year ago March.

"She had kept it on her dresser in a little sealed vial and they say it was her prize possession. Well, she sent it to your Sergeant Carter. Into the bargain, Xylo Viola wrote (the sergeant) that she was sending it to him because she wanted him to have PART of her. WOW!"

Gomer rested the letter on his knee and sighed. The romantic implications were clear to him. After all, a body did not send their appendix to just anybody.

Ray, alias Regis, banged through the door and came over to Gomer. Ray had received 8,313 letters and he considered the 13 part of that to be a bad omen. He hadn't read most of them, of course, but he had fished out one from Leafy Mae and had it, opened, in his hand. Question marks stood in his far-apart eyes.

"Hey, Gome," he said dropping his cap and dumping himself on the floor by his buddy's bunk. "Leafy says something that puzzles me."

Gomer smiled sweetly, showing his long teeth. "I'd be proud to translate if I can."

Ray opened the letter again and read aloud:

"And love may be budding between your D.I. and Xylo Viola. They say she has sent him her appendix."

A frown dented the wide space between his eyes.

"What does she mean by that, Gome?"

"YOU know. She sent him her appendix." Gomer wagged his head shyly.

Ray nodded. "But what does she mean, appendix?"

"You mean, what does Leafy Mae mean, or what does Xylo Viola mean?"

"I mean, what appendix?"

"Oh, you mean you never heard of an appendix?"

"Not the kind you send to somebody."

Gomer smiled. "Well, the kind you send to somebody is the same kind as the other kind."

Ray's frown deepened. "Well, there's the kind of appendix in the back of a book . . ."

"Lord-a-mercy," said Gomer, "I didn't know there *was* any other kind of appendix except the kind you got operated."

"Operated? You mean she sent him her OWN appendix?"

"I mean to tell you she did."

Ray swallowed hard. "From her own . . ."

"Preserved in alcohol, naturally," said Gomer.

"You mean, HER OWN ACTUAL . . ."

Gomer nodded admiringly. "Ain't that the most personal gift you ever heard tell of?"

Ray let his frown dissolve. "But why? Why would anybody want to keep an appendix?"

"Oh, they're nice. Haven't you ever saw one?"

"No. I have not."

"Me neither," said Gomer, "but I'm dying to." An idea lit in his brain. "Say, why don't me and you mosey over to Sergeant Carter's office and see if we can get a look at it. I never have seen one my own self, and I'm just afire to see what they look like, aren't you?"

"I, uh, I dunno."

"Why not?"

"Well, Gomer, Sergeant Carter might not appreciate . . ."

"Oh, now I don't mean to go in and ASK to see it. I wouldn't do that for the world . . . go poking this here old, long nose of mine into Sergeant Carter's business."

"Then how do you expect to see it?"

"Oh, why, if I was Sergeant Carter, I'd have a thing like that on my desk. It's not every day you get hold of a thing like that."

Ray shook his head. "No, I'm not game, Gomer. Besides, I don't think he'd have it on his desk."

"Betcha! They make dandy paper weights, so I've heard."

Ray was firm. "He'll just bawl us out."

"Come on. It'll be worth it."

Ray shook his head. "We don't have any excuse to go over to his office, Gomer."

"We're off duty. He can't say we're doping off."

"No, but we don't have any excuse to go in and see him."

"Yes we do," crowed Gomer. "We'll make us up a excuse. We'll say . . . we'll say . . ."

"Yeah? We'll say what?"

Gomer struggled. "Oh, we'll say that . . ." suddenly it hit him. "We'll say we come in to talk about all this mail and about as how we'll have to do something about it, or it will whip out of hand."

"It has already whipped out of hand."

"See," said Gomer. "We got a excuse."

"Oh, this mail," said Ray, shaking his pessimistic head. "Officialdom is NOT going to take kindly to this new turn of events. Morale or no morale, mark my words. Good public relations or bad public relations, patriotism or no patriotism. The Corps doesn't encourage the men to get great gobs of mail."

"Well, it don't discourage it, neither."

"No, but when the general hears how this thing has ballooned, you can be sure he'll get a headache, and when the general's head aches, our backs will be aching."

"I reckon you might be right," said Gomer. "But it beats the living daylights out of me to think what a body can do about it."

Ray moaned. "We'd better do something or this place will grind to a halt."

"I 'spect you're right," said Gomer, who began to muse in earnest about this new problem.

But it was not in Gomer's nature to let his musings interfere with his good spirits. "Well, all this talk ain't getting that appendix seen," he said. "Come on, Ray."

"Aw, Gomer."

"Ain't your eyeballs just itching to get on that thing?"

"Not ex . . ."

"Mine sure is. I have heard about them all of my life and I have heard of this person and that person having one of them, and yet, I have never got around to seeing one. Don't you just want to, in the worst way?"

"Oh, all right," said Ray.

Walking across to Sgt. Carter's office, Gomer cautioned Ray against tampering with Sgt. Carter's feelings. "Now when a body takes a shine to a girl, they don't like it for other people to go poking in. Let's don't mention a word, or let on like we even see it."

"*If* we see it."

"Oh, we'll see it."

"Yes, if it's on his desk."

"Oh, it'll be on his desk. Wouldn't you put it on YOUR desk if it was *your* somebody else's appendix?"

Sgt. Carter was at his desk and might have been writing to Xylo Viola when the two recruits sought entry and won permission. He might have been writing to Xylo Viola because he hastily stuffed the papers into his top drawer, folded his hands and waited for the men to come in.

"Sergeant Carter, sir," said Gomer as he stepped inside. "I . . . we . . . just wanted to talk to you about . . ." He came forward, his eyes sweeping the sergeant's desk. And there, as he said it would be, was Xylo Viola's appendix, gracing a stack of papers. Gomer almost burst with delight. It was littler than he had imagined an appendix would be, but then, Xylo Viola was a little girl. She would only stand about as high as Sgt. Carter's chin and Sgt. Carter was not a tall man.

The appendix was floating free, but its tiny glass prison held it centered. The bottle had been sunk into, and mounted onto, a block of shellacked black walnut. Gomer had never seen the like of it. Since coveting his neighbor's property was a sin, he tried only to admire it.

"Yes," said Sgt. Carter. "You wanted to see me? About what?"

Gomer had plumb near forgotten and it was an effort and a half to tear his eyes off the appendix, but if he stood there "gauping" at it too long, Sgt. Carter was sure to notice. Both of Ray's far-apart eyes also tore free of the appendix, although his left eye could linger longer, undetected.

"About the mail, Sergeant Carter sir," Gomer said, sneaking a little sideways peek at the appendix.

Sgt. Carter bristled with interest. "Is it getting worse?"

Ray answered that, giving Gomer another few blissful seconds of 'gauping' at the appendix. "Clubs have been formed according to the last broadcast I heard. Girls are actually competing with each other, in clubs, to see which and who can send the most mail in a week."

Sgt. Carter groaned and Gomer unfastened his eyes.

"The major will blow his top," the sergeant said.

Ray, letting his left eye wander down to the appendix agreed. "So will the colonel."

Gomer nodded: "We have a whole special detail just to cart away the letters and packages to the Red Cross and the Little Sisters of the Poor."

Sgt. Carter's lips pushed together. "PYLE. I happen to know something of what goes on at this base. Now what have you got to tell me that I don't know?"

Ray's far-apart eyes went back to the appendix. He took a quick look before he spelled Gomer, giving him a chance to look.

Ray said:

"Well, the fan clubs and . . ."

"YOU ALREADY TOLD ME ABOUT THE FAN CLUBS."

Gomer, gambling for some more time to take a few more ganders at that appendix, opened up off the top of his head.

"Well, Sergeant Carter, sir. I started this whole thing in the very beginning and so I feel sort of personally responsible about the turn things has took and . . ." His eyes darted down at the appendix and back up into Carter's steely gaze. "I, uh, well, I want to try to think of some way to get us out of it without hurting nobody's feelings. Or without creating no ill will. And . . ."

"All right. WHAT'S your idea?"

Gomer took a long look at the appendix. He could have looked at that thing for days on end. It was the most fascinating item he had ever clapped his glims on. It had more than lived up to his expectations. It had exceeded them.

Dragging his eyes off it, Gomer said: "Oh, I don't have no idea *yet,* Sergeant Carter sir, but I just wanted you to know that I'm working on it."

The sergeant's lips narrowed even further. "Oh, you just wanted me to know *that,* did you?"

"Yessir," said Gomer. "You can count on me sir. I'll do the very best I can. And I just wanted to set your mind at ease that I'm going to try to get us out of this."

"Oh, that's nice Pyle," said the sergeant, a crooked smile piercing his cheeks.

Gomer felt justified in another long look at the appendix.

Sgt. Carter's voice had taken on that fake unctuousness

that Ray recognized as pure sarcasm. "Oh, Pyle, you just don't know how that relieves me."

"Well you can count on me, Sergeant Carter," said Gomer, jerking his eyes off the appendix. Ray kicked at Gomer's foot to warn him, but Gomer had already swallowed the bait. "I'm sure glad that I could make you feel better, Sergeant Carter, sir."

Gomer edged around a little so he could look at the appendix from a slightly different angle. He wished with all his might that he could pick it up in his own hands and turn it over and look at it from all sides. "Well, I sure am working on it, Sergeant Carter."

"You just don't know how HAPPY that makes me, Pyle."

Ray knew that the rubber band that contained the sergeant's temper was about to snap, so he quickly banged against Gomer and pushed him toward the door.

Outside, Ray took a breath of fresh air. "Look, Gomer . . ."

But Gomer was frowning in thought.

Ray started to try to tell Gomer, very gently, that the sergeant was not really counting on him to solve this whole, unholy mess. He wanted to tell Gomer that the sergeant was being sarcastic. He wanted to say that Gomer wouldn't be letting the sergeant down; that it wasn't Gomer's responsibility, that what Gomer had done was innocent and patriotic and . . .

But Gomer was standing, suddenly solemn, as men galloped past under layers of packages and letters. Men who were using their every ounce of energy to keep the base from being buried alive.

"Listen, Ray," said Gomer. "I got to go over to the PX and make a telephone call. I'll be right back."

And so it was that at 3:50 p.m. on that day, a phone rang in the air-conditioned New York offices of one of the nation's major television and radio networks.

And after a bonging and clanging and dinging of coins, Gomer Pyle's voice piped:

"This here is Private Gomer Pyle of the U.S. Marines and I have got a message for the nation."

Chapter Thirteen

"COME ON THE RUN," Gomer's aunt Beulah called to Gomer's Uncle Muley. "They are talking about Gomer on the television."

"What? Gomer on the television?" Uncle Muley yelped as he scrambled out of his growing monstrosity. The pool in the backyard was now growing to measure fifty feet in length. Uncle Muley always believed in doing a thing right if you were going to do it at all.

"Is Gomer on the television?" he cried excitedly as he banged into the house.

"Wipe your feet, Mister, before you step on my good rug."

"Where? Where's Gomer?" Uncle Muley's eyes devoured the picture on their new color television set in the living room.

"Not *Gomer,* Mister. Gomer wasn't on. But they were talking *about* Gomer!"

"Oh," said Uncle Muley, his excitement diminishing only somewhat. "Well, what did they say about Gomer?"

Aunt Beulah had put her hands on her hips. "Well, I suppose you think I could *hear* with all the ruckus you were kicking up. Until you got done hollering about it, it was off."

"Shoot," said Uncle Muley.

"What little I *did* get was something about Gomer Pyle having something to say. Something important, as I recollect."

"Well, that is a fine how-do-you-do."

"Don't you fly off the handle at me, Mister," said Aunt Beulah. "And don't set yourself down on my good couch with them cementy drawers on."

Uncle Muley stumped out of the room, went into the kitchen, pulled up a wooden chair and sat himself down by the telephone. "Central," he said into the instrument, "connect me with Grandma Pyle."

"Why, hidee, Muley, how in the world are you this afternoon?" the central asked.

"Tollable," said Muley. "How is yourself, Central?"

"Well, other than this bealin' on my knee, I can't complain."

"How in the blue-eyed world did you get a bealin' on your knee, Central?"

"Bumped it agin the car door and it just bealed up."

"I declare," said Uncle Muley.

"Well, it will go down in a day or two. Lissen, Muley. Grandma Pyle is on the wire, talkin' to Pastor Goins, I think. You want to call back?"

"Sure enough. Pleasure talking to you, Central."

"The pleasure was mutual."

Uncle Muley hung up. "I was trying to call Grandma Pyle," he informed his lawfully wedded.

"I wouldn't never have guessed."

"She'll have saw the television."

"Call up Cousin Ralph. He'll have saw it."

"His set is broke."

"My stars," said Aunt Beulah coming into the kitchen and taking some cold ham out of the refrigerator. "When did his set break?"

Uncle Muley shrugged. "He told me yesterday that he had it in for repairs."

"Well, then ring up the Goodpastures, or the Hoyts. They always watch the television this time of day."

"The Goodpastures has gone to Frostboot for two days."

Aunt Beulah spanked her foot. "How come I don't never hear the news unless I worm it out of you by asking you the right questions?" She didn't wait for an answer. "Call the Hoyts then."

Uncle shook his head. "I don't want to start up with Willis Hoyt."

"Willis Hoyt is a fine, upstanding man."

"He pains my neck."

"What are you holdin' against Willis Hoyt?"

Uncle Muley tossed his head: "I wouldn't get close enough to him to HOLD *anything* against him. He's a goody-goody."

"Well, you could do worse than to take him as an example, Mister."

"Shash. Maybe Grandma is off the wire now." He picked up the phone. "Central, it is me, Muley, again. Is Grandma finished talking to the pastor?"

"She sure is. Rang off about three seconds ago."

"Put me on, then, if you'll be so kind."

"No need of it, Muley. She rang me and said to put her calls through to your house. She's on her way over there now."

Uncle Muley nodded. Grandma would be coming over to discuss what the television said about Gomer.

"Much oblige, Central, and nice passing the time with you again."

"The same here."

It would not take Grandma Pyle long to get to Uncle Muley's house. In the last few years Grandma had got queer in her ways, and she up one day and bought herself a convertible-top sports car, which she drove like a demon. Since her eyes were not what they once were, she was as likely to drive on the wrong side of the road as to drive on the right side. Everybody in town had to watch out.

She was particularly hazardous on "Corkscrew Avenue," the mountain road up to Uncle Muley's place. She usually hugged the inside lane close to the mountain and unless you knew she was coming or happened to be breaking the law yourself and driving on the wrong side, you had to move like a fox to get out of her way. So far everybody had. The Lord looks after a body when a body's going on seventy-six.

Grandma Pyle slammed on her brakes and hove up to within an inch of Uncle Muley's concrete-block pool. She slammed the car door and, cane in hand, stomped into the house.

"Hidee there, Grandma Pyle. It pleasures me a mighty lot to clap eyes on you today."

Grandma Pyle didn't answer. She hung the cane on the coat tree and stomped over to her favorite straight chair. Cushy chairs were hard on her back, but she wouldn't admit it. Straight chairs were the only concession she made to her age.

"Well sir," said Uncle Muley. "What brings you out on a day like this?" He dared not ask her right off the bat what the television had said about Gomer. Grandma Pyle did not like to rush into things. She liked to exchange pleasantries first.

Despite her penchant for driving like the wind, Grandma believed in taking things in their own time. Life, she often said, should have time in it for exchanging pleasantries.

"Well, is it hot enough for you?" she said, opening the conversation.

"I hope to tell you," said Aunt Beulah, who was now sitting across from Grandma.

"Hot enough," said Grandma, "to fry your brains in their skull."

"You can say that again," said Uncle Muley.

"Puts me in mind," said Grandma Pyle, "of the summer of nineteen-ought-three. Now that was a summer. Got so hot the ice-house flooded."

Uncle Muley began to rock in his favorite rocking chair. "How's your October beans?"

"Drooping like the ears of a hound dog."

Uncle Muley nodded and rocked. "Whut can you expect in this weather."

"That's for sure," Grandma answered.

"How's Ralph?" Uncle Muley asked, gradually edging the conversation toward family so he could ease into the subject of Gomer.

"I ain't saw Ralph since this morning."

"How was Ralph this morning?"

"Tollable. His television is broke."

Uncle Muley brightened. Ah, now the word "television" was fair game.

" What good have you saw on the television lately?"

Grandma snorted. "Not a blessed thing. I put a plate of my best pewter through the picture part last night when I got put out with one of them late movies."

Uncle Muley's face fell. So then she hadn't seen it either. But he kept trying on the outside chance. "I hear tell there was some talking about Gomer on the television a little while ago."

Grandma Pyle nodded. "I heard tell the same thing."

Uncle Muley bit his lip and had another go at it. "You got any notion WHAT it was they said about Gomer on the television?"

"Not a glimmer of a notion," said Grandma Pyle. "But whatever it was it was nice because Pastor Goins is coming up here to talk to us about some idear he has for throwing a 'do' for Gomer."

"The preacher is coming up here?"

Grandma nodded. "He will be here in a spell."

Suddenly Aunt Beulah let go with a yelp. "Why, I ought to sure enough trade my head in!" she scolded herself. "If I'm not the silly one." She got up and scurried over to the television set and went to flipping the knobs. "The other station has the news thirty minutes later, and if I had a head on me I'd have thought of it before this."

Uncle Muley jerked out his pocket watch. "Right on the nail," he said, his excitement rising. "Tune it on."

"I am tuning it on as fast as I can tune it on."

The newscaster's elongated face flashed on the screen, wobbled and assumed its normal proportions. He was talking about tax money.

"I'll bet we have missed out on it."

"Shish," went Aunt Beulah.

The newscaster left off talking about tax money and began to talk about a dust storm in Kansas.

Grandma Pyle sat attentively watching the dust storm.

Then, finally, the newscaster smiled and said: "And Gomer Pyle of the United States Marine Corps . . ."

"This it IT!" whooped Uncle Muley.

"Then, shish, so we can hear."

"We missed part of it already."

"SHISH!"

". . . the nation. The Marines are getting so much mail that Gomer says 'things are so good, they're bad!' " The newscaster stopped to chuckle at that.

"Well, get on with it," commanded Grandma Pyle.

As if responding to command, the newscaster got on with it. "Gomer praised the patriotism of his fellow Americans, and now listen to this . . ."

"We are listening, we are listening," Uncle Muley said to the box.

". . . Gomer Pyle suggests that all you good people out there who have been writing to him and to the men in his platoon . . . he suggests you write to the men in the Army, Navy, Air Force . . ." the newscaster chuckled again ". . . and even the Coast Guard. That way, Gomer says, all the boys will be getting mail and nobody will get more than he can read. OR EAT! Now, how about that for cooperation between the branches of the armed forces?

"Who said there's any animosity between the services? But for that full story, let's go to Gomer's base and our reporter, Selfridge Wickerknight."

A picture of the base headquarters flashed on the screen and under it a line: "TAPED."

Gomer's Uncle Muley jumped around with joy. "I thought you said Gomer HIMSELF wasn't on the television."

"He wasn't on the other station," said Aunt Beulah.

"All the stations do different things to get the best of each other," Grandma explained wisely.

Then, before their hungry eyes, stood Gomer, squinting into the lights and smiling.

"He has put on flesh," crowed Grandma. "Land alive, but don't he look good!?"

"Shish, Grandma," said Uncle Muley forgetting his manners. She didn't notice because they were all bent forward to see and hear Gomer.

Gomer was standing beside Selfridge Wickerknight and

the latter held a small, elongated mike. Selfridge Wickerknight said:

"Good afternoon. This is Selfridge Wickerknight. I'm here with Gomer Pyle of the U.S. Marines. Standing here in front of his base headquarters. Gomer is the recruit who started the 'Mail to Camp' craze which has swept across the country like nothing since the yo-yo craze a few years back. What have you got to say about that, Gomer?"

Selfridge Wickerknight pointed the mike at Gomer. Gomer looked at it and then looked at the camera. "Are we on the television now?"

Selfridge Wickerknight chuckled. "We certainly are, Gomer. The folks back home are watching you this very minute."

The word "TAPED" again floated across the bottom of the screen.

"Oh, goody," said Gomer, wrinkling his nose and waving into the camera. "Hidee folks. Hello family! Grandma are you looking in?"

"I sure enough AM," squealed Grandma Pyle.

"Gomer," said Selfridge Wickerknight, clearing his throat. "How did all this 'Mail to Camp' craze start."

Gomer twisted and looked into the mike as he spoke. "Well, first there was this newspaper story . . ."

Television didn't relish dwelling on newspaper stories, so Selfridge Wickerknight interrupted: "Tell me, how much mail did you get?"

Gomer was still looking into the pointed mike: "Enough to fill up a tobacco warehouse and then some."

"Uh huh, and now you want to share with the other armed services. Is that right?"

"Right as rain," said Gomer grinning into the camera again and wagging his index finger to wave at the folks back home. "All them other fellers . . ." he broke off ". . . you going to tell the folks how to get the names of the fellers in the Army and so on?"

"That's right," said Selfridge Wickerknight, facing the camera. "All the local stations on this network will give you the address where you can write for your names."

Then he turned back to Gomer. "Gomer, this is certainly a good idea of yours."

"It wasn't nothing," said Gomer, modestly. "See my drill instructor, Sergeant Carter, he . . ."

Selfridge Wickerknight cut in. Gomer was not built for short, snappy television interviews as Selfridge Wickerknight had discovered in his preliminary conversations with the recruit.

"Well, folks," said Selfridge Wickerknight, "that was Gomer Pyle, the Marine recruit who . . ."

"Wait onct," said Gomer, squinting. "Can I say one more thing?"

Selfridge Wickerknight reluctantly pointed the mike at Gomer. Gomer looked into it and said: "Listen, everybody back home. We appreciate all you done. I am writing you all a letter to tell you how much we are obliged for all them vittles and how I want you . . ."

Selfridge Wickerknight, smiling stiffly, cut in: "And so Gomer is still writing to the folks at home. And now back to John Shirtwaist in New York."

John Shirtwaist in New York came on chuckling. "Well, that was Gomer Pyle. Remember, for the address of where you write to get the names of boys in the service, keep your dial on this channel. Now stay tuned for sports and the weather."

Uncle Muley sat rooted to the spot and watched all through the weather and the sports and a commercial, or two or three, and the local station break where they gave the address of the camps where you could start sending packages and letters. He sat rooted right into the cartoon program and finally Aunt Beulah said:

"Mister, there's not going to be no more about Gomer."

Uncle Muley nodded, got up and turned off the set.

Then the three of them sat there and stared into space for a spell. Finally Gomer's Grandma said:

"Did you ever see or hear the like?"

Uncle Muley blew his nose.

Aunt Beulah dabbed at her eyes.

"Every last one of us in his family has a right to be proud as a peacock for that youngin'," said Grandma Pyle.

"He was brung up proper," said Aunt Beulah.

Uncle Muley blew his nose again and went to answer the front-door bell.

Pastor Goins waddled into the living room and said:

"Did you ever see or hear the like?"

"Not in all *my* born days," said Grandma Pyle.

Pastor Goins sat down. "Our Gomer has set a example that some of these here boys in tight pants would do well to take after."

"You can say that again," said Uncle Muley.

Pastor Goins pulled idly at his drooping socks. "I'll tell you what I have been turning over in my head. I think we ought to throw a 'do' for Gomer."

"That would be mighty thoughty," said Aunt Beulah.

"Mighty," said Grandma Pyle.

"Thoughty," said Uncle Muley.

The pastor nodded. "A sort of a Gomer Pyle Day. Sinking Springs could have a Gomer Pyle Day."

Grandma perked up even more than she was already perked up. "And we'll write to the Marines and invite Gomer's whole pontoon."

"Platoon, Grandma."

"When I want you to give me a lesson in grammar, I'll AST you to give me a lesson in grammar," she said, putting Uncle Muley in his place.

"A 'do' for Gomer would be neighborly, particularly if we invited the whole platoon," said the pastor.

"There might be a parade even," said Aunt Beulah.

"And a cake walk," said Grandma Pyle. "We ain't had a cake walk in a month of Sundays."

"Gomer will be pleased as punch," sang Aunt Beulah.

Pastor Goins got up. "I'm pleasured that you folks think it's a good idear. I'll be going along now. Think I'll drop down to the Chamber of Commerce and put the idear to them."

Chapter Fourteen

The events which transpired in the next week unfolded on several fronts.

At Gomer's base, the mail slacked off as the nation took his message to heart.

Across America the beautiful, from sea to shining sea, girls were writing to men in the Army, the Navy, the Air Force and the Coast Guard. Across the fruited plain, boxes of citrus were crated for the servicemen. Under the beautiful for spacious skies, teenagers dreamed of Army men, Navy men and men in the Air Force and Coast Guard. And America's amber waves of grain were chopped into wheat which was made into flour which was used by the mothers of America to make cookies.

Men in the Army, Navy, Air Force and Coast Guard decided, with sudden glee, that it *was* more blessed to receive.

The Salvation Army and the Little Sisters of the Poor sighed with relief. All of the branches of those two charities within a 100-mile radius of Gomer's base had been virtually inundated by the platoon's booty. The Salvation Army did not need much more salvation and the Little Sisters of the Poor were no longer very poor.

The mail orderly at the base crawled out from under, and his life drifted back into its old routine. "Hidee, there," said Gomer. "The mail has been stacked up so high in your arms lately that I had clean forgot what your face looked like."

Fat Gorley happily shoved one of his correspondents off on the Army. It was a circus fat lady who had taken a shine to his picture and who had flooded him with old circus posters and newspaper clippings.

Jim Holmes socked in to learn all he could about mortar,

the noise sending ripples of happiness through his large frame.

And Sgt. Carter gazed at Xylo Viola's appendix and dreamed of the day when he would meet her. When, oh when?

The sergeant was, by turns, grumpy as a bear, docile as a lamb, and rambunctious as a bull.

In his bad moments, doubt riddled and wracked him. How long would Xylo Viola be content with a romance on Marine letterhead? If and when he did meet her, would she like him? Would his luck break again? Would the old pattern resume?

In his good moments, his eyes swung like a pendulum from her appendix to the new picture she had sent him. It was taken at the 63rd Cawkey County Ramp Festival. He would take the letter out and read it again:

"I wrote a song for you. It is entitled 'I Have My Eye on Someone I've Never Seen.' Daddy Drum says he will get a recording made of me singing it and I am going to send it to you. Do you have a phonograph to play it on?"

Sgt. Carter wrote back that yes, yes, yes, yes, yes, he had a phonograph to play it on.

The record, however, had not yet come, and when he thought about it, Sgt. Carter's doubts redoubled and dark clouds floated across his sunny mood. Had she forgotten, lost interest? What? How long did it take to cut a record? Carter sought out a radio technician on the base and asked him how long it took to cut a record.

"Hour, maybe two if everything was set up and you went to a regular studio."

That news plunged him further into gloom. He would brighten again when the mail orderly brought letters from Xylo Viola.

"No flat package for me?"

The orderly shook his head. "Not flat. Not no kind."

"You positive?"

"Positive."

"Sure it hadn't got mislaid?"

The orderly sighed. "I'm sure."

To cheer himself up, Sgt. Carter went over to the PX to buy another present for Xylo Viola. He had already sent her a Japanese *sake* set (which she was using to keep her hairpins in); a book on judo (which she put up beside the Farmer's Almanac and the Fireside Songs book on the shelf beside her bed); a large picture of himself; a plaque with a bronzed U.S.M.C. campaign hat on it, and a den rug with the Marine emblem woven into it.

This time, as a hint, he picked out a record. On its label was: "Many records have been made about the training of a Marine . . . but never has a disc proved to be more authentic than this one." . . . *Leatherneck Magazine.*

The record promised a tempting array of sounds, including the lowcrawl through the infiltration course; the firing ranges; the tear gas chamber; the roars from the bayonet fighters and PT field; the sounds of assault by helicopter, landing craft, troopship and tank, and—most important—the shouts of the drill instructors.

The record praised itself as being "the whole story from mess duty to the Marine Hymn, 50 minutes."

Sgt. Carter romantically inscribed the gift card: "An eye for an eye and a record for a record."

Feeling better he read her new letters and let his spirits soar.

But his spirits would soar only so long as he didn't trip across some little word or phrase that could be taken more than one way. He went over his letters from her with such scrutiny that when he finished reading just one of them, he would need to wash his eyes with boric acid.

He had to know anything and everything about Xylo Viola. He even steeled himself and sought out Gomer occasionally to ask for enlightenment.

"Pyle, what are ramps?"

Gomer squinted heavenward: "Well, they are different from onions and not the same as leeks. I have heard tell they are of the turnip family but they put you more in mind of scallions." Gomer whapped his arms helplessly. "You have really got to taste one to know one."

Meanwhile in Sinking Springs, preliminary plans for a

Gomer Pyle "do" were interrupted as Gomer's letter to the church arrived. Pastor Goins, looking more chapped than ever what with the extra work he was putting into planning the "do," read Gomer's letter at a Wednesday evening's prayer meeting.

Gomer asked only one thing: That the folks of Sinking Springs set an example for the nation by writing to the boys in other branches of the service.

In the middle of all the planning, the Sinking Springs mothers sat their daughters down on the rush-bottomed chairs in the kitchen and told them to write to soldiers and sailors just to be neighborly.

And so it was that one evening as Sgt. Harold Q. Carter of the U.S. Marines, took a good-night look at Xylo Viola's appendix, a group of eager-eyed soldiers at Fort Rucker, Alabama, lit matches and crawled across their barracks floor to take one more look at the 36-inch picture of the Sinking Springs Young Women's Sunday School Class, Menlo Acuff, teacher. The picture had been sent, along with left-to-right identification, by Leafy Mae Sipe, who figured to be neighborly.

"Neighborly" was not exactly the word the men at Fort Rucker chose to describe her, but that wasn't important.

What was important was the blue-eyed corporal who gazed ravenously down at the image of Xylo Viola Drum.

"I am going to rush her off her feet," he murmured. "I am going to rush her as she has never been rushed before."

The Army was moving in.

Chapter Fifteen

The people of Sinking Springs
cordially invite your presence
at a parade, cake walk, and

eating on the grounds in honor
of Marine Private Gomer Pyle
on Saturday the 16 of August.
All day long.

The invitation went to every man in Gomer's platoon, to Sgt. Carter, and to "The Commander in Charge, United States Marines, Headquarters, Washington, D.C."

The secretary in the commandant's office bucked the invitation along to the office of public information, which received all things that did not strictly conform to all other things.

In the office of public information, a dozing Larry R. Moran finally found it at the bottom of that day's pile of the routine—letters from crackpots, and forms requesting hometown releases on Marines who had graduated from boot, won marksmanship awards, been transferred or otherwise distinguished themselves.

No longer needing to exercise whatever feeble talents he had for smelling news, Larry R. Moran did not recognize the invitation as any "public relations opportunity."

Furthermore, he did not know what to do with it. It did not fit into the category of hometown releases, and there was no file into which it could be appropriately filed so he sent it FYI (for your information) to Brig. Gen. Kenneth A. Cusps. Satisfied that he had disposed of it with the least bother possible, Larry went back to mooning about the clerk typist.

General Cusps, thinking that Larry had again recognized a good story—a story which would boost recruitment and show the humanity of the Corps—issued an order to grant all the men in Gomer's platoon, plus the D.I., a three-day special leave. Then, he himself accepted the invitation.

Word of all this reached Gomer Pyle's camp the same day it reached Sinking Springs. The folks in Sinking Springs didn't think it one bit unusual that the leave had been approved for the entire platoon or that a brigadier general had consented to attend their "do."

They were mighty pleased, but not surprised. It was all like what they had expected. It never entered their minds that the invitation could have wandered eternally, from desk to desk, logging hundreds of miles in inter-office travels in the curious, mysterious ways of a bureaucracy.

For the people of Sinking Springs, however, only God, and not the military, moved in mysterious ways.

As for the men in Gomer Pyle's camp, they were more surprised than Fat Gorley looked. A three-day leave and all those beautiful Sinking Springs dolls! They whooped and hollered and clapped Gomer on the back so often that his third and fourth sacroiliac were almost unhinged.

Then, late that night, something happened that was to make Sgt. Carter think maybe his mind was unhinged.

At 2:15 a.m. as he lay dreaming, he felt someone shaking his shoulder.

"Wake up, Sergeant Carter."

The sergeant would have known the voice if he had been stone deaf, but he clung stubbornly to his dream.

"Wake up, Sergeant Carter. It's me, Gomer Pyle. I know it's against regulations to creep around in the night, but I just had to talk to you. Hope you'll forgive me this one time, Sergeant Carter. . . ."

Carter snorted awake, briefly flailed his arms and snapped on the lamp. "Wuuuuuuuuu?" said the frog in his throat. He bounded up on one elbow, squinting to dispel the film over his eyes. "PYLE, WHAT'S HAPPENED? WHAT'S WRONG?"

"I can't sleep," said Gomer. "I been thinking up a storm."

Carter switched back his cover and jerked his legs over the side of his bunk in one fast motion. He was really too delighted over the prospect of seeing Xylo Viola to work up a fit worthy of his name, but he took a stab at it:

"Pyle, are you off your rocker?"

"Far as I know, I'm sound of mind," said Gomer. "We ain't had a looney in the Pyle family since my great-great-Uncle Gideon. And they was them as said Uncle Gideon was crazy like a fox. He just up and quit working one day.

Said 'This is darn foolishness.' Never worked a lick nor turned a finger from then to his dying day and he lived to 101."

Carter got up slowly and waved his hand in front of Gomer's eyes. "Pyle, are you walking in your sleep?"

"No sir. Go on and pinch me. I never did drop off to sleep tonight. I been so busy thinking in my head."

Carter groaned. "I must be dreaming this."

Gomer shook his head. "No sir, you ain't dreaming. But I know just how you feel being woke out of a sound sleep. Hard to get your bearings. I have the same fault myself, if you can call it a fault. Once our barn caught fire in the middle of the night and I slept through the whole thing. Yet, to this day, they tell me I was in the bucket brigade and led the horses out and everything."

"PYLE! Did you wake me up just to chew the fat?"

"Oh, no sir. I come to tell you something."

Carter massaged his head with both hands. "All right," he snapped. "But spit it out and spit it out fast. Fast, fast, fast."

Gomer shuffled his feet. "I might need more than ONE sentence to get the whole thing said," Gomer warned.

Carter ground his teeth. "Abbreviate it. Just get to the HEART of it, Pyle. The HEART of it."

"Oh, I can get to the heart of it in one sentence, Sergeant Carter. The heart of it is that I ain't no hero."

"Swell, swell," said the sergeant, longing to tune back in on his dream where it had been interrupted for this special announcement from Gomer Pyle. "I am very happy you aren't letting all this hero talk go to your head, Pyle." The sergeant urged one eye fully open and let it glare up at Gomer: "NOW GET BACK TO YOUR BARRACKS BEFORE I WAKE UP AND CLAP YOU IN THE BRIG!"

"But I ain't told you what I come in to tell you," Gomer bleated. "I come in here to say that I'm not going to just sit still for that ceremony honoring me in Sinking Springs. Why, they are putting me up for a hero and it wouldn't be honest for me to sit still for all that honoring. I ain't no hero."

Carter was suddenly and fully awake. He hadn't been more awake since the night in Greenwich Village when he had been mooning after a waitress and had swilled four large cups of expresso coffee before she introduced him to her husband.

"What Pyle? You don't want to be honored? Why? What is not honest about it?"

"Oh," said Gomer. "Wouldn't be fair for me to just set there and take praise that I don't deserve."

The sergeant yelped: "But the *people* think you deserve it."

"Don't make no never mind," said Gomer. "*I* know I don't deserve it. I know it in my heart, and that's where it figured on shaving the whiskers off my face, I had better be counts. My Grandma Pyle always said that as long as I able to face up to a looking glass." Gomer shook his head, "No, just setting there and letting them put me up as a hero would be the same thing as selling day old eggs for fresh. Same as watering the milk. Same thing as . . ."

Carter waved the recruit into silence. He had to think, and his head was spinning crazily. If Pyle wasn't going to let them honor him that meant that the whole weekend would be cancelled. If Pyle wouldn't go along with the ceremony, the whole thing was off.

So *this* was the turn his bad luck with women would take this time! A recruit stumbles over his conscience, and Carter's romance goes under. Carter kicked himself for not guessing this wrinkle in advance. He just hadn't been thinking. Had he stopped for just one minute to consider it, he might have guessed that Gomer would balk. Gomer with his modesty. Gomer with his painful, literal, infuriating honesty. Gomer with his straight and narrow ideas of what was right and what was wrong. He should have known. All the clues were there. Gomer had been strangely silent all day. It had been the others who had made the noise—enough noise to please even Jim Holmes who was a generous contributor to the uproar.

Gomer opened his mouth to say something but the

sergeant barked him into silence. He had to think. This was a turning point in his life. The timing was crucial. It might already be later than he thought. Timing was essential with women. He couldn't risk any more days having Xylo Viola running around free and unspoken for. He simply had to get to Sinking Springs and Gomer's ceremony was the only hope. Carter thought frantically. He turned the rulebook upside down in his mind but nothing shook out of it that helped him.

There was nothing in the Marine Manual which could force a Marine to accept an honor bestowed by civilians. Pyle couldn't be ordered to go to Sinking Springs. Not even the general could order him to do it. And when Gomer got righteously stubborn like this, it was next to impossible to get him to change his mind.

Gomer had been silent as long as he could stand it. "See, you and me both knows I'm not that good of a Marine to be a hero."

Carter, who in happier days would have been delighted to agree, now turned on the roasting spit and faced the idiotic prospect of saying nice things about Gomer. But to get to Xylo Viola Drum, he would gladly have nominated Gomer for President of the United States.

"Pyle," he said, straining all of the acid out of his voice and steeping it in confectioner's sugar. "You did a good thing when you asked the people to write to the men in the others branches of the service. A good, patriotic thing."

Gomer blushed. "I'll remember you saying that to my dying day. Coming from you, that's a real compliment 'cause I know how honest and truthful you are, Sergeant Carter. But it still don't make me no hero. I still can't take praise for being a hero."

Carter writhed. No, diplomacy wouldn't work. Praise was no good. Threats of violence were out. Carter was in a mental minefield. Trickery was his only hope. He would outwit Gomer, out-think him, out-maneuver him. Somehow, someway. He would trick Gomer into changing his mind and going through with the Sinking Springs ceremony.

Carter took stock of his own skills. He had learned

strategy in combat, cunning in judo, slyness in field games. He would use all of his skills in this war with Pyle. If logic did not convince Gomer, strategy would surprise him, cunning would outwit him. Pyle was a raw boot; Carter was a man with sixteen years in the Corps. He fired his first volley:

"Pyle, the men are counting on this."

"Oh, yes. I know that."

"And the men are your friends."

Gomer grinned. "I'm mighty proud of that."

"And you don't want to let them down, do you?"

"Oh, no sir."

Carter stormed through this opening in Gomer's defense line. "Then, you'll go through with the hero bit?"

"No sir. It wouldn't be right to put myself up as a hero."

Carter fell back, regrouped and sent in fresh troops. "The people of Sinking Springs are counting on this."

Gomer shuffled his feet. "But it's THEM, the people of Sinking Springs, that ought to be honored and not me! See, they did all the cake baking and package mailing. They was the patriotic ones. It's them as deserves honoring."

Sgt. Carter spied a weak point in Gomer's right flank. Craftily he eased around and moved in. Sinking Springs was Gomer's weak point. He would hit him there.

"I had always thought, myself," said the sergeant, "that *we* really ought to honor the people of Sinking Springs."

Gomer blinked.

Carter pressed his advantage. "Pyle, why couldn't we have a ceremony to honor *them?*"

Gomer jumped around on one foot. "And you'll make a speech to honor them, Sergeant Carter, and . . ."

"Oh, well now, I don't know about making any speech," said the sergeant. Making speeches terrified him. Next to women, public address was Carter's most singular non-accomplishment.

Gomer's face fell. "Oh, but you'd have to make a speech, Sergeant Carter. For it to be right."

Marring what he otherwise considered to be a textbook victory, Carter took the casualty of making a speech and agreed to this term in Gomer's surrender.

"All right, Pyle," he said. "I'll make a speech."

"And tell them as how I don't feel right about being made into a hero when it is them all along that is the heroes? It is them ought to be honored. And that we aim to do just that and honor them."

"Yes, yes," said Carter, licking his wound but congratulating himself on his own shrewd tactics. Mentally, he stood with his foot on Gomer's neck. "Pyle, you'll agree once and for all, then, to go to Sinking Springs?"

"Oh, sure, Sergeant Carter."

"Good, good," said Carter.

"Oh, I'm just so happy," Gomer bubbled. " 'Course we will have to give them some sorty gift. Something patriotic and all."

Carter nodded. "You give that some thought, Pyle."

"Oh, I have been," said Gomer. "I been thinking about it all day. In fact, that's why I couldn't sleep, thinking about this whole thing."

Now Carter blinked.

"Thinking about WHAT WHOLE THING, Pyle?"

"Oh, about us honoring them."

Carter felt strangely lightheaded. He squinted like a mole in the sunlight. "You mean . . . ? But I thought you were ready to call the whole thing off . . . why a few minutes ago . . . you . . ."

"Call it off? Oh no, Sergeant Carter. With all them people prettying up the town and all. And with all the fellers having their mouths set on going. Oh, no I wasn't about to call it off. What give you the idea I was aiming to call it off? Furtherest thing from my mind."

Carter's eyes were both spinning in different directions. "Pyle, you said . . . your exact words were that you weren't going to SIT STILL for being honored."

"Yes sir. And I don't aim to set still for it. I aim to stand up and honor them right back. I aim to put them straight on this hero business."

"But, but, you weren't going to go through with this ceremony at all . . . I distinctly heard you say you weren't going to go through with it."

"I just don't express myself as good as you express yourself, Sergeant Carter. But what I meant was that I was just not going to set still and take any honoring without standing up on my two feet and returning the compliment and honoring right back. Otherwise it wouldn't be honest. But me honoring them just wasn't good enough. YOU have to honor them."

Carter bit his cheek. "Pyle, why didn't you tell me this in the beginning?"

"I tried to. I come in to tell you that I wasn't no hero and that I wasn't going to set still for being honored. I was also going to tell you I thought we ought to have a special honoring ceremony for the people, but you took the words right out of my mouth and *said* that we should have an honoring ceremony for them. Then, you agreed to the speech and all. Wouldn't have been right without you making the speech. Wouldn't have been official for just me to stand up there and honor them. And you agreed to it right off. But I knew you would, Sergeant Carter. I knew you would."

Chapter Sixteen

FOR THREE DAYS in advance of the Gomer Pyle "do" the water pressure in Sinking Springs reduced itself to a dribble.

Until they found the reason for it, folks was mystified . . . good and plenty.

Roy Goodpasture's wife stood trying to rinse a fork under a trickle of water as slender as the thread in her sewing machine. "I declare, Roy," she said. "I bet the weeping willows has got their roots into the sewer pipes again."

Xylo Viola Drum, who had been washing her hair daily

since news of the impending arrival of Sgt. Carter, stood soapy-headed under the weak gurgle coming out of the shower head.

"Daddy Drum," she called in her mellow alto. "Are you watering the front lawn grass? The water in here is plumb tuckered out."

Leafy Mae Sipe put her delicate paw under the spigot, turned it on full blast and watched the little wire of water struggle forth. "Pop," she called. "Go and run a snake through the pipes."

Pastor Goins had to wait at his faucet in the church for ten minutes to get enough water to sprinkle on the head of an infant girl baby, in for baptism.

And Grandma Pyle, who had decided to wash her sports car so it would be pretty for Gomer, stamped her foot in disgust as her garden hose oozed a miserly sum of water, such a little bit, in fact, that it fed back along the hose. "Why this here water's git-up-and-go has got up and gone," she mused, leveling a beady eye at the hose. "Now, I just wonder . . ."

She turned off what little water there was, got into her sports car and baroomed up Corkscrew Avenue to Uncle Muley's place.

"Muley," she sang out as she stopped her car two inches from his front porch. "Get around here. I want to do some talking."

From the sound of her voice, Grandma Pyle was going to slice all the fat off her conversation. There would not be time for any pleasantries today.

Uncle Muley high-tailed it around to the front and stood waiting for Grandma Pyle to give it to him.

Pointing her cane at him, Grandma Pyle said: "Muley, are you filling up that dang swimming pool of yorn?"

Uncle Muley nodded his head sheepishly.

"Well, what have you did? Have you put a extra pump on that hill? The town is drier than a Sunday sermon."

"Now, Grandma . . ."

"Don't you now-Grandma me. They ain't enough water for me to wash off my car for Gomer."

Uncle Muley hung his head. "I wanted to fill up the pool for Gomer."

This stumped her momentarily. She blinked, opened her car door and, cane in hand, stomped around to the back where water was gushing ferociously into Uncle Muley's olympic-size, hand-made, concrete block swimming pool.

She leveled a trained eye at the size of the pool and multiplied in her head. "You turn that water down to half and it will still get full time Gomer comes."

Uncle Muley hemmed. "It's a big old pool, Grandma Pyle."

She nodded firmly. "It'll fill. Now, you go and cut down that water to about one half."

Fitfully he walked over to the tap and under Grandma Pyle's stern gaze the water slacked off to about the size of a small girl's thigh.

"That is still a stack of water," she snapped. "I said half."

"That IS half."

"Half nothing. That is three quarter. Now, Muley, you cut it down to half and no more muling around about it. A body would think you had more sense in your head. What were you thinking of, anyhow? I thought you was brought up better."

The water reduced to the size of a girl's wrist. "I didn't know it was depriving nobody."

"Didn't know, my foot. You know good and well that when you put a extra pump on that hill, even for a hour or so, the town dries up like a bone."

"Well, I was thinking of Gomer."

That always got to her. "As it is," she grumbled as she watched the healthy stream of water, "folks'll be all day drawing a good size tub."

The martyr sighed. "I betcha it won't fill time Gomer comes."

"It'll fill," said Grandma Pyle, who had now turned Uncle Muley around and was pushing him into the house. "Now you get yourself on the horn and tell the telephone central what you done. Come on now, Muley."

"Aw . . ."

"No awing about it. Get on that horn and tell before folks get the water works people up here after you with shotguns."

Uncle Muley grudgingly picked up the telephone.

Grandma Pyle sat down on a straight chair in the kitchen and looked around, taking in the automatic stove, automatic ice box, automatic disposal, automatic can opener, automatic dishwasher. But as long as the kitchen still had a good "country" smell to it, she didn't disapprove. She sniffed. Yeast. Beulah was about to bake bread.

"Central," said Uncle Muley into the telephone. "I want you to get on the party line, if you would, and tell one and all why the water pressure is down."

"Is yours peaked too, Muley? Land, I ain't seen the like since the reservoir ran dry."

"Well, it is because of me," he admitted.

"You? What in the world you a'doing, Muley?"

"Filling up my swimming pool."

"Law, I should of guessed. When did you finish it off?"

"Week ago Monday, but just running a hose into it didn't fill it fast enough."

"I'll bet you anything that you are filling it up for Gomer."

Uncle Muley nodded. "I have turned down the water so as to give the other folks more," he said sadly.

"How long will it take to fill, Muley?"

"From the looks of it now, a hound's age. I got the water turned down so low now that it don't amount to a hill of beans."

"Will it be full time Gomer comes?"

Uncle Muley let his lips droop. "Prolly not."

Grandma Pyle, once the conversation began, had cocked her ear against the earpiece so as to hear both ends of what was being said, grabbed the instrument from Uncle Muley and held her firm hand over the talking part.

"You had good-and-well-better tell her that it WILL be full if you expect folks to tolerate this. Folks is not going to tolerate having their pressure as weak as all get out unless it is for a worthy cause."

Uncle Muley nodded and took back the receiver. "Yes, it ought to get full time Gomer gets here."

"Tell her definite that it will be full by that morning," Grandma Pyle rasped.

"It will definite be full by that morning."

Central giggled. "Then, Gomer and that platoon of his'n can take a dip after all the speechifying."

Uncle Muley brightened a little. "That was the general idear."

"Oh, how plumb nice."

"Yes," said Uncle Muley. "I want you to come up one of these days too, Central, and have yourself a dip."

"Aw, Muley, I don't cut a very fancy figure in a swimming suit."

"What's the difference? We are all home folks up here."

She giggled again. "Well, maybe one of these days. I bet that pool is a sight."

"Prettiest thing you ever did see." He jiggled happily. "Spruces up the place. Sets it off, like. Takes your eyeballs off that dang litter all over the mountainside."

"Oh, that old Pugh place ought to be tore up."

"You can say that again," said Uncle Muley. "Anyhow, will you spread the word, Central?"

"I sure will."

Uncle Muley's concession to Sinking Springs' water plight helped Xylo Viola get her hair washed without so much fuss and bother, gave Roy Goodpasture's wife enough water to execute her offices, insured the baptism of all the new little girl babies, and let Grandma Pyle get her car washed.

But with his water coming in at one-half its previous rate, Uncle Muley fidgeted and fussed that it might not fill the pool by the time Gomer came.

After supper that night, he looked out and noticed that the drag of washing the town's supper dishes had cut his half-ration of water to a third. During the commercials on television all that night, he got up, looked out, and mournfully noted that the toilet traffic was reducing his pool's intake to two-thirds of its half-ration.

Then, just before bedtime, when everybody washed his teeth and tubbed and all the rest, Uncle Muley's pool had to muddle through on one-quarter of what Grandma Pyle had prescribed.

With his weakened demands upon it, the water pressure wasn't staying in his pool. He shouldn't have listened to Grandma Pyle. But he knew better than to cross her.

He picked up the calendar as if that would help matters and ran his finger under the three scant days remaining: August 13, 14 and 15. Gomer would be here on August 16.

"Come on pool," he said. "All I ask of you is to be full by August 16." Then he cocked his head and added:

"August 16 of THIS YEAR!"

Chapter Seventeen

AUGUST 16 WAS NOT only anticipated by Gomer's platoon of Marines. The date also had a joyous ring to it for a company of Army men in Fort Rucker, Alabama. August 16 was the day they were to move out in convoy heading north to Pittsburgh, where they had been reassigned.

They would move up, clogging the highways and frustrating the late summer tourists with their snail-like strings of jeeps and trucks. They would bump over the small state roads and eat the dust of detours. They would endure heat that Satan himself would be hard put to emulate.

Even so, all of that was a delightful prospect when compared to not moving at all. The trip would be an adventure in discomfort but almost any discomfort was a number of cuts above the discomfort of staying in Fort Rucker.

Fort Rucker is not known for the devotion it stirs in the hearts of the men stationed there. In fact, what the army men say about it is hardly fit for a sailor's ears.

So the prospects of moving out struck joy in the approximately 200 hearts thumping inside the approximately 200 breasts of the Army's hard-fighting finest.

One of the hearts belonged to Cpl. Sam Fynes who had drawn himself temporary duty at a typewriter in Lt. James Lascomb's office. It wasn't a bad hitch, but then Sam Fynes was usually lucky that way. Lt. Lascomb was a nice guy even for an officer. A product of ROTC, the lieutenant had a Ph.D. in the Philosophy of Science, hardly a skill the Army knew how to use. Since no one understood what the philosophy of science was, Lt. Lascomb had been assigned to office duty in the troop control center.

That was fine with him. He was only serving out his obligations and marking time until he could get out of the Army and teach. As a result, it was fairly easy to wheedle things out of him. Like most philosophers, the lieutenant was slightly glassy-eyed and preoccupied.

He was moving out, too, and would ride in the advance column with the other officers. However, he was too intrigued with a new scholarly treatise on space and time to care much about moving out.

Sam came trundling into the office from chow and sat down at his typewriter. He noticed that the maps had arrived and that the orders were ready to be typed. Sam rolled his handsome blue eyeballs over the instructions and fed a sheet of paper into his typewriter. Then he studied the map.

The map had been wounded by a tortuous and squiggly red line which snaked up through the south to Bristol, where it steadied, somewhat, on Highway 11, and then, from Breezewood on, shot almost like an arrow across the Turnpike to Pittsburgh.

"Wham," said Sam Fynes. "Did you see how they routed us through the south? Every dinky back road in this part of the Confederacy."

The lieutenant grunted.

Cpl. Sam Fynes shrugged. "Since it is the most illogical way to go, I suppose it is therefore the only normal way for the Army to go."

"Yes," said the lieutenant, who readily agreed that the Army's logic did not conform to any other kind.

Cpl. Sam Fynes began to type. "I'm bringing up the rear as usual. I'll be eating everybody's dust."

The lieutenant looked up. "Oh, the units—whatever you call them—will be far enough apart so you won't be eating any dust. You'll be about six hours behind the —uh—what do you call it?"

"Advance column."

"Ummm, yes."

Fynes began to type again, breaking into the lieutenant's thoughts on Euclidian geometry once more with: "Hey, we bivouac the first night out. TVA property . . ." Fynes' eyes grew wide as beachballs. "WOW OH WOW OH WOW."

Since a bivouac on government land is neither unusual or thrilling, Lt. Lascomb looked up to see if Sam Fynes had hurt himself. "What's wrong? Bite your tongue?"

Cpl. Sam Fynes had not bit his tongue. He had just seen that the bivouac area was six miles north of Sinking Springs off Highway 66.

"SINKING SPRINGS," he whooped. "SINKING SPRINGS! SINKING SPRINGS."

The lieutenant had not kept up on the latest slang so he assumed "sinking springs" to be just another one of those mysterious terms the young use.

"We bivouac near Sinking Springs, Lt. Lascomb! Sir."

The lieutenant put the book face down on his desk. "Oh, so Sinking Springs is a place?"

"Is it EVER a place. I've got a girl there." Sam Fynes snatched the map to his breast, lept up from his chair and raced over to show the lieutenant the flyspeck on the map. "Oh, golly, Lieutenant. I've just got to see her! You suppose you could spring me? I mean it IS done on convoy in SPECIAL cases and this is a SPECIAL case! A very special one."

"I don't see why not," said the lieutenant. "I'll tell the captain that I gave you my special permission."

"Oh, Lieutenant!" yelped Cpl. Fynes hopping on one leg. "This is beautiful. This is just too beautiful!"

Lt. Lascomb picked up his weighty tome again and indicated with his eyes that he was very anxious to resume his reading. Fynes, however, hung fast by his superior's desk. "Uh," he said, interrupting again. "Uh, is it okay if I have one of the men in the advance column tell her that I'm coming?"

The lieutenant sighed. "Why not just write a letter, Fynes?"

"Oh, sir, Xylo Viola might not get it on time. The mail into Sinking Springs has been all fouled up lately."

"All right. Go tell one of the privates in the lead jeeps to see me about it."

"Oh happy day, oh sweet 16 August. Xylo Viola, honey, here I come, baby."

"What's her name again?" asked the lieutenant.

"Xylo Viola Drum. She's musical."

"Sounds musical."

"She is also a winner. A real winner."

So was Sam Fynes. Winning ran in his family. In World War II, Sam's father had received the Purple Heart by catching his finger in an adding machine. Sam's mother had won the family car in a raffle.

Sam's winning specialty was women. He had always been successful with women.

At the tender age of two he had clapped his lean little hands on a sun-suited contemporary, and she, with love in her eyes, had made him a gift of her sand-bucket.

The pattern hadn't altered much in the nineteen years that followed.

It wasn't hard to see why. Cpl. Sam Fynes was pretty hard to resist. He was six feet tall, and muscular. He had even white teeth, blonde hair, blue eyes. And his timing was just flawless.

Chapter Eighteen

AUGUST 16 DAWNED GRADUALLY. As the sun slowly came up in Sinking Springs it brought the morning glories to life out of their twirled buds and gently blessed their spent sisters who had awoken the day before and now curled their puckered lips upward.

The hollyhocks beside Uncle Muley's store wore their blooms like garish crepe-paper hats.

Main Street had been washed (albeit slowly with the water pressure still ailing), and the sidewalks swept. "NO SPITTING" signs bobbed like gay, yellow bibs on the parking meters.

The air was sweet and fresh, having been washed by a shower the night before. The grass was bright green, even where it poked up between the cracks in the sidwalks.

Over in the Sinking Springs High School football field, where the parade would disband, a temporary reviewing stand had been erected. Built of green lumber, its tangy smell mingled with the mothballs of the patriotic red, white and blue bunting looped over, under and around it.

A banner stretched over the main entrance along Highway 66. There had been a large hassle some days earlier over what wording to use on the banner and a number of lifelong friendships had threatened to collapse.

Of all the versions of what the banner should say, the one that was finally agreed upon, Pastor Goins intervening to prevent bloodshed, was "WELCOME BELOVED LEATHERNECKS."

Flopping and billowing over the highway, the banner would be the first thing the boys would see. Or almost the first thing.

Uncle Muley grouchily proclaimed that Gomer would

first see that dang Pugh place on the mountain. The banner would help to offset that.

If you stood under the banner and looked down the highway toward the way they would be coming, Uncle Muley's ridge was just down a little ways and off to the right. It reared up majestically, with his property hanging out slightly like the bunion the ridge was named after. Of course, stringing down the side of the ridge for most of the 650 feet of its height was the Pugh place junkyard.

The folks did as much primping with that banner as they might do with one of their girls who was setting out on her first date. With girls outnumbering men the way they did in Sinking Springs, a first date (or a date of any kind) was nothing to sneeze at.

The folks looked at the banner from the coming-in side. They walked down the highway to the place where they could look straight up and take a chance of having Uncle Muley spit in their eye.

Then they would walk up and look at it from the other way. From behind, it jiggled and flapped over the highway, which stretched down and away in a squiggly line—south—Highway 66, the main road and the only road into Sinking Springs from the south. It was the same road, unbeknownst to all, that a company of army men were cursing as they barreled north.

Gomer and the boys were due in at 1:00 p.m. which meant that if you wanted to be on hand at the city limits to clap eyes on them the minute they came into sight, you had better plan on being there at noon because there was quite a bit of confusion over whether the Marines were on daylight saving time.

You could stand right by the city limits sign which said "SINKING SPRINGS, DRIVE SLOW" or next to the boulder which bore the chiseled words: "PREPARE TO MEET GOD."

Them as wanted to be really sure of being there early enough to see Gomer, not trusting clocks or daylight time, set their minds at 11:00 a.m.

But Gomer pretty near tore the transmission out of

the jeep and highballed it there at 10:30 passing unnoticed under the banner and barreling out Hay Fork Road to deliver Sgt. Carter to the Drums, who were expecting him for lunch.

The Drums lived about a mile and a half out from the tobacco warehouse in a two-story white frame house which sat back about the distance of a good city block from the road.

Their mail box was the shape of a large musical note —the note formed the circular base; a steel rod connected the note with the staff, which was for the mail. Five words, whittled out of wood, announced the proud ownership: "Home of the Singing Drums."

The jeep kicked up a rain of gravel as it spun into the winding driveway. Gomer yanked at the hand brake and said: "Well, here we are, Sergeant Carter."

Hymn, Lord bless him, the Drums' one and only son, a feisty seven-year-old with a thatch of butter-yellow hair had stationed himself by the open window in the front room. Sighting the jeep, he burst immediately onto the porch and although he looked straight at Gomer, he yelped:

"Daddy Drum, Daddy Drum! GUESS WHO IS HERE!"

Daddy Drum, still in his undershirt and suspenders came bounding through the door, ignoring M'am Drum's standing rule about letting the screen door slam. Once on the porch, Daddy Drum stopped stock still. "Bless my socks," he said to Hymn. "Way you was yelling, I had the notion Gomer must be here."

"He is, he is, he is," Hymn screamed with delight, playing his daddy's straight man.

Daddy Drum turned all the way around and went to looking under the swing and behind the porch chairs. "I sure as the dickens don't see him nowhere."

"There, there," yelled Hymn, jumping around on one foot and pointing to the pleased and blushing Gomer.

Daddy Drum blinked. "You don't mean to tell me that there handsome feller is GOMER PYLE."

"Yes, yes, yes!" Hymn was delirious, his yellow hair flopping as he danced with glee.

"What? That feller is Gomer? That feller in that there neat uniform, standing up straight as a ramrod? That there feller with shined shoes on his feet?"

"The same, the same," crowed Hymn.

Daddy Drum, scratching his head and playing this for all it was worth, warily approached Gomer. "Come up here, young man," he said to Gomer. "Turn around once."

Daddy slapped his head again. "Well bless my eye-sockets. If it AIN'T Gomer! Gomer, you are plumb handsome. Why, the Marines has done you good and helped you, too."

If Gomer's smile had been any longer it would have got hung up in his adam's apple.

Daddy Drum turned to Sgt. Carter. "And you must be the sergeant," he said, making a fairly safe assumption since the sergeant was the only other man in sight.

"Shake hands with Sergeant Carter," Gomer said to Daddy Drum.

Daddy Drum put a wringing grip to Carter's hand. "Well, I've heard a heap about you, all of it good."

Turning back to Hymn briefly, Daddy Drum said: "Let's see, Hymn. Now, which one of my feet is better than the other one?" Daddy Drum studied his feet. "Do you favor the right one or the left one?"

"Why, why?" giggled the well-trained straight man.

" 'Cause your mama said for me to put my BEST foot forward for the sergeant."

Gomer doubled up. "Oh, that is a good one."

"Listen," said Daddy Drum, "let's get on inside before we take sunstroke. Them women SAID they'd be ready in a jiffy which MEANS that they won't be ready for a spell yet. Gives us some time to shoot the bull."

"I thought you shot the bull yesterday," Hymn said, feeding Daddy a line.

Daddy Drum snapped his fingers. "By granny, you're right. Reckon we'll just have to settle for talking."

When Gomer got done laughing at that one, he told Daddy Drum that he had to scoot. "Nothing would pleasure me more than to set a spell, but my family'd skin me alive. I better high-tail. If they get wind I stopped ANYWHERES ELSE first they'd be fit to be tied."

Daddy Drum slapped his head again. "Bless my button-top shoes if you don't speak the truth." He pushed Gomer toward the jeep. "I don't want it on my head. You better git."

Gomer ground the jeep into gear and after a few "see-you-all-laters" left in a storm of gravel.

"Now there," Daddy Drum told Sgt. Carter as they watched Gomer lurch out of sight, "there goes a good old boy. They broke the mold when they made that youngin'." Sgt. Carter secretly thanked his stars for that.

On the steps of the porch Daddy Drum suddenly stopped, swooped around, drew himself up to his five-foot-four-inch height, made a courtly bow and elocutionated:

"Come on in and meet the Singing Drums. We're the sassiest, brassiest, wing-dingiest singers in Cawkey County. We grab notes from the treetops and toss them at the sky. We wrassles with guitars and twangs up a storm. We rip into them banjos and strum up a twister. We toot our trumpets until the foothills shiver. We raise our voices and the jackpines splinter. We're the Singing Drums. Boom! Boom!"

Sgt. Carter looked at him in astonishment, but speech finished, Daddy Drum changed his tempo again. "Let's git on in and meet up with the family," he said joyfully, opening the screen door for the sergeant and Hymn to enter. "Hurry up before we let the flies in," he cautioned Hymn.

Daddy Drum, a short, bouncy man with thinning straw-colored hair, waved Sgt. Carter into a chair and whipped up a trumpet lying on the piano in the corner of the living room. He went to the foot of the stairs and sounded an introductory blast which caused Carter to grab at the chair arms.

"RA-TA-TA-TA-TAH-TAH!"

"Guess who's here!" he bellowed, following that with a few bars of the Marine Hymn.

"Hold on to your horses," came an off-stage feminine voice which made Carter's heart leap into his mouth.

"All the same to you," yodeled Daddy Drum, "I'd druther hold on to that high note." He gave out another sharp bleat.

"Well," he said, exercising his embouchure and wiping his mouth with the tips of his fingers. "That ought to put a hustle into them." He came over and sat down opposite Sgt. Carter.

So much had assailed Sgt. Carter's ears that he had not had much time to exercise his eyes. Now, looking around, he became aware just how much the house reflected its master. A raised platform near the windows formed a small stage on which reposed an assortment of musical instruments, including the upright piano. Behind the piano, curtains billowed gently inward brushing the keys. The pattern printed on the curtain material was that of singers, eyes lifted and mouths open. A life-size tuba, cast in plaster of Paris, served as a planter which bloomed with African violets.

An end table, carved out of black walnut, was a king-size harmonica. A picture on top of the harmonica table caught Carter's eye. In it, Daddy Drum stood hand outstretched toward an assortment of little girls, all with harmonicas. Around the room on tables, hung on walls and marching across the mantel were family pictures, most of them taken on stage at various periods in the development of the Drum girls. Toward the end of the mantel an infant Hymn put in a photographic appearance in his daddy's arms under a banner which said "Jethro Barn Dance."

Daddy Drum, seeing the path of the sergeant's gaze, leaped up and began to dart around, collecting the framed pictures in his arms. "Here," said he, descending on the startled sergeant. "This is us at the county fair in 1952. That little tyke is Xylo Viola. And here," he said sweeping another picture into the sergeant's hands, "is us at the Cawkey County Revival in 1955. That's Xylo Viola."

He kept handing down the pictures until Sgt. Carter's

arms and lap were full of them. Then, cocking his head, he responded to a light coughing sound at the head of the stairs and leaped over to the piano.

"In-tro-doo-cing the SINGING DRUMS. BOOM, BOOM. Purtiest ladies ever to come out of Adam's rib. Purtier than the blushing rose, sweeter than the scented honeysuckle. Ladies and gen . . . uh . . . pardon me . . . no ladies in this audience . . . GENTLEMEN, May I present the Singing Drums."

Sgt. Carter sat glued to his chair as the tune of "When the Saints Come Marching In," rippled off the keyboard and the Drums came marching down in order of seniority. Mam led the troupe, then came Melody Belle, Xylo Viola, Clara Nettie, Mandy Lynn, Reveille Lullabye, Organ and Harmony Carol. As each came into sight, Daddy sang her name.

Sgt. Carter struggled to get to his feet, but the lapful of pictures had him snowed under. When he tried to move they clacked together ominously and dug their sharp edges into his arms.

Onto the stage skipped each of the Singing Drums. When all were in place, Daddy Drum sounded a large chord and they launched jiggily into:

> Welcome Sergeant Carter, welcome to our home
> This is but a starter, sit, no need to roam!
> Welcome Sergeant Carter, welcome to the Drums,
> Set, we'll entertain you with songs and tunes and
> hums.

Daddy Drum and Hymn now joined the ladies and added a bass and a shrill soprano to the proceedings.

> "You are our pride, you bring us joys
> In the uniform of the leatherneck boys.
> We're proud to have you, it's good to know
> God will bless you, where'er you go."

Then they picked up the chorus:

> Welcome Sergeant Carter, welcome to our home...

When it was over, the Drums broke their pose and fluttered over to help the dumfounded Sgt. Carter out from under the pictures.

"You must be the sergeant," said Mam, shaking his hand warmly. "Welcome, welcome, welcome." Then over her shoulder she said: "Daddy Drum, go on up and put on your shirt. You look like a hired hand sitting there in your undershirt and suspenders."

Daddy Drum laughed: "Well, the show must go on. Feller don't always have time to climb into costume."

Xylo Viola stepped forward and said in her low, melodious voice: "It's so nice to meet you in person, Sergeant."

There she stood before him, her brown eyes gazing at him. Xylo Viola in the living flesh, all pink and cream, all soft and embraceable. She was even prettier than her picture. Carter just wanted to grab her and carry her away to some deserted island. Instead he just gulped, felt himself get moist and warm all over, and listened to himself sink into a monosyllabic mumbling.

Xylo Viola was a little shy too, at first. It was hard to realize that the person you had said all those things to in letters was really this same person you were clapping your eyes on for the first time in your life. Just before lunch, though, she began to chatter brightly.

For lunch they were seated around a dining room table which was in the shape of a grand piano.

Carter sat at Daddy Drum's right, across from Xylo Viola. Separating Hymn from the sergeant would have required major surgery, so he was allowed to sit at the sergeant's right. They sat down to an empty table—but not empty for long.

Mam came out of the kitchen at the head of a phalanx of girls bearing the meal. Platters and dishes were set on the table. There was baked ham, glazed with pineapple juice and brown sugar and studded with nut-brown cloves; white potatoes, sweet potatoes and squash which was the same color as the sweet potatoes; green pole beans with a few crimson-striped shelley beans tossed in for color; fresh sliced crisp cucumbers, large sliced red beefsteak tomatoes, golden corn on the cob, ruddy-red radishes, home-canned piccalilli, bread-and-butter pickles, crab apples and watermelon rind; buttermilk biscuits and pale yellow sweet butter and ice tea in pitchers beaded with cold droplets.

Mam apologized for having only one kind of meat, explaining they generally ate light on Saturday because Sunday's meal was so big. She also apologized for the biscuits which she said weren't as fluffy as they should be. She started to apologize for a few more things, when Daddy Drum silenced her by announcing grace.

When Daddy Drum cleared his throat after grace, that was the signal that it was all right to start. Before Carter could lift his prayerful head, his clean plate was visited by a three-inch slab of ham. Someone put the gravy bowl in his hands.

"Please pass the biscuits," Daddy Drum told Sgt. Carter. Balancing the gravy bowl in one hand, Carter reached gingerly for the biscuits. Then, suddenly, plates began to spin past him faster than he could focus on them.

With dizzying speed, mashed potatoes and sweet potatoes flew past; salt cellars were exchanged and replaced; butter was sliced off and hot ears of corn whipped through his hands. Dishes reversed and came back again. He had barely had time to scoop out some beans before the squash and the pickles were in his hands. He was behind and once out of step, it was impossible to close the gap. He soon realized, however, that it didn't matter if you didn't help yourself on the first turn around the table, because the circle was repeating itself. Round and round again came biscuits, mashed and sweet, gravy, beans, pickles, relish, tomatoes, cukes, salt, butter, crab apples, radishes, the gravy, the corn, the mashed, the sweet.

Carter switched his head from left to right until his Eustachian tubes were unequalized.

Suddenly it stopped, and all bowls were soundly thumped down on the table. All were set.

All but Mam Drum. She put her napkin to her lips and

clucked. "Land sakes alive. But I almost forgot my special surprise for the sergeant." She leaped to her feet.

"Oh, mama," said Xylo Viola with a slight bit of embarrassment for her parent. "The sergeant don't want no ramps!"

"How do you know what he wants? Are you inside his head?"

The Drums howled with glee.

"Well no, but . . ."

"Now, Sergeant, you were asking about ramps weren't you?" she said, not waiting for his answer.

Carter sipped his iced tea and drank in Xylo Viola who was saying: "She meant you were curious about ramps."

"Oh, yes, yes," said Carter, still not knowing either what he said or did.

Xylo Viola said: "See, ramps are . . ."

"Please pass the red-eye," Daddy Drum said to Sgt. Carter.

"The red-eye?"

"Gravy."

"Oh, yes, sure thing."

"Anyway," said Xylo Viola, "Mama just wants you to see ramps . . ."

Mam fluttered in from the kitchen with a plateful of fresh ramps. "There you are," she said, placing them before the sergeant. "I had Hymn pick them just for you."

"Butter," said Reveille.

"Say please," Mam corrected.

"Those ramps," said Xylo Viola. "Ramps are . . ."

"Butter, *please*."

Sgt. Carter passed the butter.

"Now, ramps . . ." Xylo Viola tried again.

"Hymn," his daddy sang out, "don't bump your heels against your chair like that."

"Ramps . . ." said Xylo Viola.

"Biscuits, please," said Melody Belle.

"Ramps . . ."

"Hymn, eat something besides your sweet potato."

Sgt. Carter picked up a ramp.

"Wait," cried Xylo Viola.

"Reveille, get your elbow off the table."

Carter chomped into the ramp. Then politely chewing it he proffered the dish to Daddy Drum.

"Oh, no thank you."

Across the table he offered it to Xylo Viola.

"Thank you kindly, but no."

Carter offered it to Hymn.

"Nup."

"None for me, thanks."

"No thank you."

The ramp had a pungent taste, but Carter hardly noticed it. He only noticed Xylo Viola's eyes, Xylo Viola's lips, Xylo Viola's hair, Xylo Viola's teeth.

He did not even notice that Daddy Drum had begun listing heavily to the left away from Carter. Hymn was listing heavily to the right—also away from Carter. Xylo Viola just gazed at him with a melancholy look in her big brown orbs. Carter downed another ramp and mooned back at her.

After the dessert of black-bottom pecan pie and ice cream molded in the shape of a harp, the Drums left the table, and Xylo Viola invited the sergeant to "take a little walk."

Merrily caroling "Don't step in the cow pies," she led him away through the fields.

From the kitchen the clatter of the Drums' seven female dishwashers drowned out everything else they said. Mam and Daddy watched from the porch until they were out of sight. "Well," said Daddy, winking at Mam, "I hope Sergeant Carter ain't got his heart set on getting kissy-face."

Mam looked startled. "I should hope *not*. He only just met her."

Daddy Drum sat down beside her on the porch swing. "Is that why you fed Sergeant Carter the ramps?"

"What? What are you talking about? Minute they get alone, your mind flies to kissing. And what has that got to do with ramps?"

Daddy Drum drew out his pipe and began to fill it. "Did you ever kiss *me* when I had just ate ramps?"

Mam ducked his probing gaze. "Well, so what if they don't go to kissing first crack out of the barrel?"

Daddy leaned toward her. "Aha! So you did do it purposeful?"

Mam moved irritably, causing the porch swing to jounce. "I didn't give no mind to it one way or the other. Kissing never entered my head."

Daddy struck a match and sucked it into his pipe. "Sergeant Carter sure is a nice feller."

Mam gave the swing a sharp little push with her foot. "Of course he is. And I like him a lot, but I *don't like* the tone you are taking."

"Who, me-me-me-me . . ." sang Daddy Drum.

"It might be of interest to you," she said, "to know that kissing is not the only thing young people think about."

"I got news for you."

"Now you stop playing the fool with me, Jubal," she said, ominously using his given name. "Besides there is no big thrashing rush. I didn't let you kiss me until the third time you took me out."

Daddy Drum snorted so hard he blew all the tobacco out of his pipe and had to get up and stamp at it. "I kissed you silly FIRST time out," he said, patting the embers with his toe.

"You didn't even hold my hand until the second time out."

"That is correct. But I kissed you silly first time out."

"On that hay ride? You did not."

"Well, I sure as the dickens kissed the fire out of somebody."

Mam sniffed. "Your memory is failing." She sighed. "Besides, young people today go rushing pell-mell into everything. Sergeant Carter and Xylo Viola have got plenty of time to decide if they like each other."

Daddy had filled his pipe again. "Umm, hmmmm," he said between drags. "I just made mention of the fact that

Sergeant Carter smells to beat the band and won't get a crack at being kissy-face today."

"Well, tomorrow is another day," said Mam shading her eyes to see what was coming up the long gravel driveway. Daddy Drum flicked his match over the porch railing and got up. "Looks like Gomer is coming back. It's a jeep."

"If that is Gomer, I'll eat a ramp," said Mam, as the jeep skidded to a stop and a soldier jumped out.

Daddy Drum was already down the steps. "What can I do for you, son? You one of Gomer's boys?"

Pvt. Johnson of the U.S. Army screwed up his face. "Come again?"

"You one of the Marines?"

"Marine!?" The boy shook his head. "I've got a message for Xylo Viola Drum. She live here?"

"She's out right now," said Mam from the porch.

"Well, I have a message from Corporal Samuel Fynes of the U.S. Army."

"Oh," said Mam, her hands fluttering like birds. "That's the nice little army boy that has been writing to Xylo Viola."

Pvt. Johnson wasn't interested in Sam Fynes' virtue or size. He had orders from Lt. Lascomb to deliver a message. "Well, will you tell her our company is in convoy and is going to bivouac here tonight, and Corporal Fynes says to tell Xylo Viola Drum . . . She your daughter? . . . that he'll see her around supper time."

Daddy Drum nodded. "Be proud to tell her," he said. "But won't you come in, Private?"

"Would you like a ham sandwich and a glass of iced tea?" said Mam coming down the steps.

"Uh, no Mam. Thank you very much. But I have to get to the bivouac area. You'll tell your daughter that Sam Fynes will be here?"

"Sure enough will," said Daddy Drum.

The young private hopped back aboard his jeep, and waving, spun away in a fit of gravel.

"When it rains," said Daddy Drum fingering his thinning straw-colored hair, "it pours." He put his arm around

Mam. "Now, Xylo will have two swains courting after her."

"Good healthy competition," said his wife, "is the American way. It never hurt nobody yet."

"Ummmm."

"Besides," said Mam. "The sergeant out-ranks the corporal."

Daddy Drum hoisted an eyebrow. "He out-RAMPS him, too!"

Chapter Nineteen

A Sinking Springs parade wasn't worth "boo-turkey" unless it got a little bit snarled up before it got started. If it got rolling on time, it meant there wasn't a *whole lot* to get rolling. And the Gomer Pyle parade had a lot to get rolling.

The floats and the marchers started assembling on the north end of town where Highway 66 snaked northward in reluctant search of Yankee land. The meeting place was the C & S Grocery & Service Station. The platoon, which had scattered itself over the face of Sinking Springs in pursuit of its womanhood, had no trouble finding the C & S because it was the only grocery and service station at that end of town.

Brig. Gen. Kenneth A. Cusps, who had flown in, had been met by the mayor at the County Airport, and the mayor had directed him to the official car, which was really one of the demonstration models in one of the local showrooms. The mayor's chauffeur wasn't really a chauffeur; he was Horace Groiner, the truck farmer who was more accustomed to driving a tractor and who was quite apprehensive about chauffeuring a general.

He needn't have worried. The general smiled broadly and clapped the mayor on the shoulder. "I thought you would be a whole lot more folksy than this, Mayor."

"Well, this is quite an occasion."

The general laughed. "I don't stand on much ceremony," he said. "Here, let me drive." Thus he relegated the startled mayor to the seat next to him and commanded the relieved Horace to the back seat.

So, everybody got to the C & S more or less on time. But that only added to the confusion. There were more bodies and vehicles than the parade marshal could keep track of.

The parade marshal was Fire Chief Len Welt, a tall fellow with no chin and a neck that fed right up out of his collar and into his face. He was busier than a man with two snakes and one hoe.

One of the high school kids had misplaced a tuba and one of the Cub Scouts was throwing up. Worse, Grandma Pyle had materialized on the scene and had gone to insisting on driving her sports car in Gomer's parade. Chief Welt, who didn't have any hair to tear out, elbowed through the mess in search of Gomer Pyle, who did have hair to tear.

He asked Sgt. Carter if he'd seen Gomer.

Carter, who was guarding his mouth with his cupped right hand, like a man who had just had all of his teeth pulled, shook his head "no" and headed again for the men's room at the C & S.

Carter had bought a small toothbrush, a traveling tube of toothpaste, some Sen-Sen, some peppermint drops and a bottle of mouthwash.

He had little time either to be irritated with the delay in the proceedings or to worry about his speech honoring the folks of Sinking Springs. A bigger problem was tying up all of his circuits. Ramp breath, he was discovering, was indelible, like ink that won't erase. He was doing his best to wear it out, but he couldn't tell if he'd made any progress. This, coupled with the onslaught of the army corporal—calculated for supper time — caused him such acute pain that he could not suffer more than in those two directions at the same time. In his mind's eye, he saw his romance sinking like an anvil in a swamp.

Chief Welt ploughed through the tangled crowd looking for Gomer. To let Grandma Pyle drive in the parade would be to sanction disaster. She'd ram the car in front of her which would then ram the car in front of it, and on it would go. Somehow they had to find a place for her in one of the other cars.

But he couldn't find Gomer. Each time he asked somebody, they said: "Sure, yeah. Gomer was just here a second ago."

Finally, making a complete, if elliptical circle, Chief Welt came back to where he had started and there was Gomer talking to his grandmother. And his grandmother was having none of it:

"Gomer Pyle. Don't you tell me what to do in a parade for my own grandson."

Gomer was hangdog. He turned to Chief Welt. "She'll only ride if she rides with Ray," was his dismayed report.

Grandma Pyle had taken an immediate shine to Ray because of his far-apart eyes. "Democrat," she whooped. She locked her eyes onto his wide-set glimmers and pronounced that not only *he,* but his entire family was Democrats. In fact, to have give birth to Ray, she said, "They's not been a soul in his family to vote gee-oh-pee in 75 years." She nodded affirmatively. "Not for him to have eyes that far-apart there ain't been."

She was, then, willing to ride, if she rode with Ray. But Ray was not riding. He was marching with the platoon. Efforts to appease Grandma Pyle by putting her in the mayor's car only made her more adamant. She had taken it into her head that the mayor's granddaddy had voted for McKinley and although no proof of this was to be had, she wasn't about to change her mind.

For a little while, the hope went up that she would consent to riding with the general, but the general, leaping at the opportunity not to be driven, even slowly in a parade, had announced that he would lead the platoon in its march.

Sgt. Carter came back into the fray chomping Sen-Sen, but he paid little attention to what, if anything, was being decided. He leaned against a truck bed and licked his wounds. He hadn't gotten within ten feet of Xylo Viola when he had finally managed to get alone with her. Ten feet was still better than a few hundred miles. And ten feet shot him through with delight. That is until the news of the Army's imminent arrival. Some army men had already rumbled through town. Xylo's correspondent was due at 4:30 or 5:00. He mused painfully on Xylo Viola's fluttery excitement at this news. Like biting down on a bad tooth, he relived it. He got mad at her and forgave her all in the same instant, all in one heartbeat. It was only natural for her to be flattered, he said to himself, as he nurtured homicidal thoughts about the army corporal.

He popped some more peppermint into his smarting mouth and moaned. The old pattern. He should have known. He should have left those nine perfumed letters in his wastebasket that morning not so long ago. He was marked for failure with women. If there was any doubt before, it should be clear now.

"Oh," he groaned. "Oh, oh, oh."

"Oh," came the echo from Chief Welt. "Oh, oh, oh!" Chief Welt was beside himself. "We've got to work up a whole new line of march," he said profesisonally. "Listen. Listen, EVERYBODY. *Listen here, now.* PEE-Ple is waiting!"

Indeed they were waiting.

Along Main Street and across Bama Run Road, up Duck Foot and over to the football field, folks waited in the hot sun for the parade to begin.

Some roosted on old apple crates and blew their noses over the sidewalk. Some jounced crying babies until the infants fought for wind to cry with. Most stood, three deep.

The kids sat on the curbs. Most of the kids were small girls, because girls, small or otherwise, was what Sinking Springs had the most of. They sat with their knees up to their chins, their legs splaying down like two sides of a triangle and their feet, pointed inward, forming the base.

Men moved their toes inside of their hot heavy shoes

and the beads of sweat from their brows dropped and sizzled on the hot pavement. Women, with talcum powder on their faces and arms, sprouted little blisters of sweat under the powder, and sported little crooked paths of perspiration on their carefully primed countenances.

The stores were so empty you could have shot a cannon through them without hitting a soul.

On the jam-packed sidewalks, rumors of the parade's start were a source of constant furor. Kids continually leapt to their feet with shrill cries of:

"Here it comes!"

Once, it actually did look like it might be coming, but all that came was a moth-eaten old dog, loping sideways. In the process of crossing the street, it became aware of the attention focused upon it, and like all creatures, became suddenly vain. Realizing it was in the limelight, it got a smile in its jaws and trotted, cross-legged and haughtily to the end of Main Street where it rolled over on its back, hoisted one leg toward its Maker and let its tongue loll out.

Somebody finally shooed it away, and it got up, scowling and limping at the injustice of fleeting fame.

Then, without warning, here it did come. HERE THE PARADE DID COME! The colors, borne by the American Legion hove into sight, the ex-soldiers, grunting under the weight, stumping down Main Street. Now fat and fiftyish, the Legionnaires seemed to be punctured in the middle by the stob-ends of the flags. And they carried them flags like they was aiming to ram down the door of city hall. Stump, stump, stump, they came.

The mayor in his open demonstration convertible was next. Although there was more than a few in the crowd who had seen the mayor and chatted with him that very morning in the feed store, all eyes strained to drink him in . . . all necks craned for a better vantage. He waved and shouted homilies and the crowd roared with glee. Even if you knew him well enough to know which brand of snuff he favored, when the mayor was in a parade he was SOMEBODY.

The same went for the other local people who marched

by in disorganized little clots under banners which announced their affiliations. "Sunshine Ladies Sewing Circle" was in small letters under a big sun, stitched onto an old sheet.

SINKING SPRINGS HIGH SCHOOL PTA struggled by in health shoes and some high heels, clipping and clacking and straining not to show how much their feet hurt.

The Cub Scouts had a banner which honored Gomer as their "HONORARY" den master.

The Women's Good Deed League of the Sinking Springs Community Church hoisted a bed sheet which urged: "FOR PETE'S SAKE DO SOMETHING GOOD."

Most of the floats were fairly undisguised truck beds covered with funeral home grass from Purkeys.

"THE SEPTIC TANK CLEANING SERVICE IS GLAD TO SEE GOMER."

The Dixieland Paper Company rumbled by under its slogan: "IF YOU'RE LEFT HOLDING ONE OF OUR BAGS, IT WON'T BREAK."

On it went. The seed store, the dry goods house—all had trucks or at least cars with streamers made from crepe paper.

Each was cheered. Each was a sight to see.

Oh, and then, bright-eyed and bushy-tailed came the Sinking Springs High School band, out of tune as usual but a pride and joy of the highest order. Two of the Drum girls, better trained than the rest, struggled to play out of tune to keep in off-tune with the others.

All preened and sour-noted and hop-scotched past. Fat kids, skinny kids and teenagers with raging pimples. They whinged and dinged and rooty-tooted. And they was not a spine in the hot crowd that was not accosted by chills.

Sinking Springs' two fire engines, including the new one with the 97 foot ladder, rolled past, their drivers beaming proudly from their sudden seats of fame.

The six garbage trucks, jerking and jouncing past, empty and clean but still bearing slight traces of their occupational aroma, sported proud drivers who just that morning had examined and fondled all of the town's watermelon rinds, ham bones and fish heads. Now they smiled down from their high positions on the makers of all the mess.

Cheers went up to hail these noble men, and they bowed in their trucks to those who had created the melon rinds and the fish heads and the ham bones.

Next, swinging in brisk step around the corner, came Gomer's platoon, which would have been first if it hadn't been for all the confusion back at the C & S Grocery and Service Station. It was just as well, because it was the best part of the show and the folks in Sinking Springs always liked to save the best for last.

Everybody hiked their children up a little higher so they would be sure to see. And everybody screamed and hollered greetings to the platoon. Even Gomer Pyle resisted the temptation of rolling his eyes to the side and waving.

The platoon was led by the general. Sgt. Carter marching along side was holding something under his tongue so that his face looked long. But it was a real sight to see with them marching past like that, not a soul of them out of step.

It was not until they drew along broadside of the crowds that anyone noticed Grandma Pyle. In perfect step she bounced along in her cotton housedress.

Gomer's Uncle Muley poked Gomer's Aunt Beulah. "Shut my mouth," he said. "If that ain't Grandma Pyle. What is she doing?"

"What does it look like she's doing."

By now everyone had seen Grandma and a wave-like murmur was undulating through the crowd. "Well, ain't this a day to remember!" crowed Uncle Muley. There was Grandma Pyle marching sharp as you please beside the wide-eyed Ray.

"Wait until next time she complains to me about her lumbago," said Gomer's Aunt Beulah.

The crowd whooped and cheered but Grandma obeyed orders and kept her eyes straight ahead.

"Next thing," said Gomer's Aunt Beulah, "she will be

lying about her age and trying to join up to the Woman Marines."

For Grandma Pyle the day was clearly made. She bounced along, swaggering her gray head every now and again. The crowd couldn't get enough of it and surged along to keep the platoon in sight for as long as it could, cherishing every precious moment. This would be talked about for a month of Sundays, if not longer.

The parade's end was signaled by the inevitable collection of small girls and boys who ran, jumped and hopped in the platoon's wake.

The crowd, as one, surged toward the Sinking Springs High School football field for the speechifying.

As the parade disbanded on the field, Sgt. Carter slid over to one of the lemonade stands, secured a paper cup full of the sticky liquid and shot under the bleachers to brush his teeth. Midway in this endeavor, a small boy popped up from nowhere, and seeing Carter, stopped cold. The child looked at the frothing mouth of the sergeant and gaped in fright.

"Was you bit by a mad dog, mister?"

Carter, who had temporarily begun to get nervous about his speech in addition to all else that pained him, dispatched the lad with a growl.

In the bleachers, Uncle Muley, wilting in the heat, thought of his swimming pool — longingly, then apprehensively. It must be just about to the top by now. "I've got to git," he said to Aunt Beulah. "Save me my seat. I'll be right back."

He was not right back. He was not even back in time to see Gomer get up and protest being called a hero. He was not even back in time to hear Sgt. Carter's platitudinous remarks. Nervous as he was, Carter took it as a good omen that his ramp breath did not wilt the microphone.

Uncle Muley was not even back in time to hear the impromptu speech by the general, in which the word "patriotic" was used 99 times by count. Nor was Uncle Muley back in time for the presentation.

The Marines presented the town of Sinking Springs

with a new flagpole for the football field to replace the one which had replaced the one smashed by Horace Groiner's tractor on the courthouse lawn.

Re-enacting a slightly modified Iwo Jima flagpole raising, the men succeeded in tapping every tear gland in the bleachers. Even the general was blowing his nose. There they were, Ray-jus Ray, Fat Gorley, Jim Holmes and Gomer pushing that pole into place and unfurling the new flag, a special gift of General Cusps.

"I wish the Red Chinese could see this," Roy Goodpasture's wife said to Aunt Beulah. "I'll bet they'd change their tune."

It was to this teary, emotion packed throng that Uncle Muley returned on a dead run. Streaking up to the grandstand, he bolted onto the boards and darn near upturned Pastor Goins who was just raising his eyes to heaven in preparation for the benediction.

Jostling the surprised pastor aside, Uncle Muley put a half-nelson on the mike and belched into it:

"She's going. I tell you my swimming pool's going. She's beginning to crack. Sumbuddy better throw up a road block."

Nobody waited to hear more. In a stampede of spinning legs, folks bolted for the gate and high-tailed it for the block and a half to the city limits where Gomer's banner waved, forgotten, and where there was a good view, from a safe distance, of Big Bunion Ridge.

Reaching the city limits the crowd lifted its eyes to the top of the ridge. As if responding to a cue, there was a "KUSH" like a muffled cannon. Shading their eyes, the folks saw a blue tongue of water shoot out with a huge smacking sound.

"Oooooooooooooooooooo!"

B O O M !

Jim Holmes shuddered with delight.

The top of Bunion Ridge seemed to blow apart, and down the mountainside came a silver sheet of water on which concrete blocks tumbled as effortlessly as if they had been wood shavings.

SHOOOSH
WUMP
SPANG!

The silver Niagara surged into the old Pugh place, the grubby eye-sore of Bunion Ridge, the dumping grounds for all creation. With a mighty vaaa-ROOOOM, the white-capped silver sheet and the concrete blocks hurled themselves at the old Pugh homestead, the listing cow barn, the bones of the two trucks, the mounds of empty, rusty beer cans, the dilapidated chicken house, the discarded bottles, the hollow milk shed, the rusty auto fenders, the wheel-less baby carriages, the moldy sofas, the incapacitated three-legged tables and one-legged chairs, the dented hub caps, the eroded zinc washtubs, the stripped auto tires.

With a vigorous swoop, the silver sheet embraced the entire Pugh farm litter, engulfed it in its water bosom, wrenched it from its moorings and began to fling the whole mess down the mountainside.

Hundreds of beer cans hit trees, ricocheted off tree trunks and shot up into the air, describing graceful arcs and showering the hillside like a sparkling fireworks display.

Down came the old Pugh ancestral home, turning end on end, finally kicking free into the air where it wheeled like an unwieldy kite before exploding into a thousand pieces.

"Ahhhhhhhhhhhhhhhhhh."

"Yipppppeeee," roared Uncle Muley, dancing on one foot.

Down the mountainside came the white-capped, concrete block studded silver sheet. Riding the crest, whipping merrily along, came the rusty bed springs, the crumpled auto fenders, the rotting lumber.

CHING BOOOOIING went the old truck bones, mobile for the first time in years. Thumpity thud went the sofas and the leggity-peggity tables, and snap whap went the one-leg chairs.

Over it all was the growing thunder as the silver sheet grew wider and stronger, fed by the broken lip of Uncle

Muley's pool and reinforced by uprooted shrubs, small jack pines, boulders and tree stumps.

In a magnificent ROOOOOOAAAAARR, it picked up speed.

Overhead, the birds wheeled and swooped, blinking their birds' eyes at this astonishing sight and dodging beer cans. Jack rabbits scooted away, racoons scrambled up trees, field mice and ground hogs zipped away from the lacy fringes of the silver sheet.

"Caw! Caw! Caw!" scolded the black crows.

"Wooooooooooooooooooo."

"Hoooooray," sang Uncle Muley.

The silver tide hung up momentarily in a thicket of trees, the huge pile of debris before it forming a temporary dam.

Then with a convulsion that shook the ground all the way back to the city limits, the churning, surging silver tide shouldered loose hurling its junk in graceful loops over the white-capped froth.

Oh, what a wonderful day! What a stupendous show! What a glorious sight!

The mountainside was a glistening shimmer of splendor. Sunlight danced zanily on the cascading water, sparkling and winking with a thousand reflected lights. Blue and white fountains leaped up, snatched a rainbow of colors from the sunlight and whirled and dashed downward.

Tumbling black tires spun out, and bounding as if being chased, turned lopsided cartwheels in the air. Concrete blocks, aided and abeted by the momentum, gouged into the earth like square corkscrews, hurling up great slabs of mud.

"Zeeeeeeeeeeeeeeeee!"

Down and down it came, slathering Highway 66 with mud, junk, tree stumps, concrete, lumber, cans, glass, tin, boulders, iron bones, and rubbish.

Suddenly, then, the mountainside was at rest and Uncle Muley's pool only drooled from its swollen lip like a wound still pumping, but controlled. An old garbage can lid whuppered around on the highway, staggered and fell, finding peace. Cleansed and bathed, Bunion Ridge emerged fresh, if frowsy, from its gigantic bath.

The mountainside, like a bather, appeared to have dropped its dirty clothes at its feet—in a tangle.

Bushes and trees bobbed back into place, shaking the beads of water out of their hair.

Uncle Muley was dancing on one leg. "If I'd have knew that swimming pool wouldn't hold, I'd of built it ten years ago. Twenty years ago!!" He feasted his eyes on the wreckage of the Pugh farm, now mired in muddy drifts which must have measured as high as twenty feet in some places across Highway 66. The highway was hopelessly blocked, maybe for as long as a week.

From now on, all landslides, all floods, all earthquakes would be measured, and probably found wanting against the day Uncle Muley's swimming pool broke. The people stared silently at the colossal heap of rubbish which now strangled Highway 66. Looming up on that highway, hulked the leavings of the Bunion Ridge mountainside, an impregnable barrier.

Only the wheeling, cawing birds interfered with the dwindling sound of the trickle oozing from Uncle Muley's late pool. Then a new sound was heard throughout the land. It was not the cooing of the turtle dove, but the squawk of the walkie-talkie.

A tall, goggle-eyed lieutenant stumbled into the crowd. "Thought it was a sonic boom," he mumbled.

The walkie-talkie answered in a scratchy voice.

The young lieutenant, an army fellow, didn't seem to know much about working the instrument but a private was helping him. The two of them made their way through the crowd and surveyed the shambles.

"They ain't going to be able to make bivouac," said the private. "This is the only road into here from the south. They'd have to go 90, 95 miles out of their way to bivouac north of here."

Lt. Lascomb, who had been roused from a dissertation on the new mathematics, nodded. He hauled out his map. "Let's see, a detour will put them . . ."

"State 33 eventually runs into 11. It's the only way. Otherwise they'll be all night getting here."

"Yes," said the lieutenant, "an unnecessary expenditure of energy and time."

"That's the way it stacks up to me," said the private.

Lt. Lascomb bent to the business of re-routing his troops, none of which could care less except one, a certain Cpl. Sam Fynes.

Sgt. Carter, recognizing the hang-up as his salvation, grabbed Xylo Viola's hand and towed her with him over to the scene of his competition's undoing.

"Trouble, Lieutenant?" said Sgt. Carter, allowing his face to break into a helpless grin.

"I'll say," said the lieutenant, taking a swift glance at the Marine dress-blues. "I have to re-route the whole tail-end of my convoy, Ensign."

Carter looked over his shoulder to see if the Navy had landed. "But there isn't anything else to do, Ensign, not with that highway in that impossible state."

"Oh, no, no," said Carter, enjoying his new "rank" in a rival service. "You are perfectly correct in re-routing your men."

"No other way," said Lt. Lascomb.

"Positively not," said the temporary ensign.

Lt. Lascomb bent to delivering this news into the rasping walkie-talkie, as Sgt. Carter popped two more peppermints into his mouth and bent closer to Xylo Viola. She didn't seem to mind. He must be wearing out the ramps. He bent even closer to say:

"Xylo, honey. This means that the soldier boy isn't going to make it."

She did not appear to be hearing a word he said. She was just looking into his eyes in a way that was melting his bones.

And so as the sun scarred the Sinking Springs twilight with a last slash of crimson, the new flagpole in the football field caught the dying blush and held it like a fiery stalk.

Across the ridges, the leaves sank from green to violet and then to purple.

In the Sinking Springs Community Churchyard, the strings of overhead lights blinked to life, except for the bad bulbs, and Gomer Pyle stood with his hands full of fried chicken and rolled his pleased eyes over the contentment that spread itself around him.

His heart as full as his stomach, Gomer reflected happily on the day's events. Every man, woman and child in Sinking Springs had enough to talk about to occupy them until doomsday. Uncle Muley had got rid of the old Pugh place and Aunt Beulah, no secret about it, was just as happy to be shut out of the swimming pool.

Gomer angled his head to the left where Grandma Pyle was digesting her supper and lighting a pipe in an attempt to create her own smog problem.

The Marines, off to the right, seemed to be well in hand. The general was sitting with the mayor and feeding on sweet potato pie. Jim Holmes was lying on the grass and letting a girl tweek his nose with a daisy stem.

Fat Gorley seemed to be winning in a three-legged sack race even though his partner in the burlap bag was Horace Groiner, the tractor driver and not the world's swiftest runner.

Ray was counting Leafy Mae's fingers and feeding her a deviled egg.

And Sgt. Carter was taking a lesson on the playing of the sweet potato from Xylo Viola Drum, who had announced earlier that she would have him playing it by nightfall.

Gomer swivled around to see how that lesson was coming.

It wasn't. Xylo Viola Drum and Sgt. Harold Q. Carter were no longer sitting beneath the old elm tree.

They had gone somewheres.